STAR WARS

QUEEN'S HOPE

STAR WARS

QUEEN'S HOPE

Written by

E. K. JOHNSTON

PRESS

LOS ANGELES · NEW YORK

Printed in the United States of America

First Edition, November 2021

1 3 5 7 9 10 8 6 4 2

FAC-021131-21260

ISBN 978-1-368-07593-0

Library of Congress Control Number on file

Reinforced binding

Design by Leigh Zieske

Visit the official *Star Wars* website at: www.starwars.com.

To all of the queens who are fighting alone:

Baby, you're not dancing on your own.

Once there was a girl who had nothing, and she was not content.

Hers was a hard world, and bleak. She grew up surrounded by dust and dereliction and was always hungry because there was never enough to eat. She sweated uncomfortably as she worked under the desert suns and froze in the night when the heat evaporated. Her family was gone, and there was no one to comfort her from the time she was small.

But the girl did have something, a belief that no one could take from her. She had faith in the inherent goodness of the galaxy and the forces that made it work. Though no one cared about her feelings or her future, she cared about the people around her, and she showed them in small ways. She didn't know it, but that made her special. Another person might have turned under the same pressure and known only hate. She was forever generous, forever offering help to those who needed it, because she couldn't keep her spirit contained.

As she grew older, she learned more of how the galaxy was supposed to work. The Jedi and their crusade to maintain balance. The Republic and its laws that couldn't protect her. What she got instead was one criminal after another, those who used their power to serve themselves only. Another girl might have given up, resigned to her fate and made bitter by it. She knew many who had, and she didn't blame them. They did what they needed to do to survive. But there was something in her that always turned away from darkness, no matter how tempting it was.

The girl got older. The desert lined her face before its time and cracked the skin of her hands. She worked endlessly, even tinkering with projects on her own time to fend off the loneliness. She could sell her work, though she would never have enough money to buy her freedom. No one noticed her, at least no one on Tatooine.

It wasn't something she heard, not exactly. It was a call, but it was the sort of call you feel. Somewhere, out in the galaxy, something was waiting for her. She didn't understand it, and she didn't have a lot of time to try to figure it out, but when she dreamed, she heard a song and she felt less alone.

The song promised her something that, for a time at least, would be only hers. There would be no ownership, no pressured obligation. Only love and connection and the sense of a home. The girl didn't feel manipulated, even though the power that sang to her was beyond her perception.

The girl knew that nothing was permanent. Even the scars on her back could be properly healed if anyone cared enough about her to do it. She was being offered a chance for joy, a chance to belong to someone because she chose to, not because she was stolen. A chance to have someone who would look up at her and feel love. Something worth fighting for.

Shmi Skywalker held out her hands to the stars and said: "Yes."

CHAPTER 1

For one of the very few times in her life, Padmé Amidala had no idea what to do. She kept secrets all the time, but this one was different. Usually, the girls she shared her secrets with also helped her keep them. They weren't just her confidants; they held her web of secrets together. And this time she was alone.

A faint whirring from the corner of the room reminded her this was not entirely true. There were other beings who would keep this secret with her, though not very many. The only problem was that none of them could help her right now. At least, she was pretty sure. It never hurt to ask.

"I don't suppose you know anything about dressmaking?" she asked the little blue R2 unit.

He turned his dome back and forth, mimicking a humanoid shaking their head, and beeped perhaps more sorrowfully than the situation really called for. Padmé thanked him anyway. There was no reason to be rude.

She returned to the contemplation of the fabric in her lap. There wasn't enough for a whole new dress, but she hadn't been expecting that. The cloth had been in her family for several generations, each person given a piece of it to incorporate into their wedding clothes. Her sister, who had chosen not to marry, had used her portion to make clothes for her daughters, showing that she welcomed new additions to the family.

It hurt, a little bit, to be doing this alone. Anakin didn't understand, but she couldn't really expect him to. He understood family, of course, and wanting to maintain a tradition. It was clothing he was a bit less familiar with. She appreciated that his compassion led him to give her time and space to work on a solution, though. They were in a bit of a hurry.

R2-D2 chirruped again, and when he had her attention, he projected a holographic image between them. It was familiar art, one of the windows from Theed palace that had been replaced after the Battle of Naboo. This one featured her, when she was queen, surrounded by orange-cloaked handmaidens. The droid's suggestion was clear.

"I can't, Artoo," Padmé told him. It caused her nearly physical pain to say it. "What we're doing has to be a secret. I can't bring them into this."

The projection changed to a holonet image taken during the victory celebrations ten years ago. Queen Amidala stood in white next to the Gungan leader, Boss Nass, surrounded by members of her court. R2-D2 zoomed in on one handmaiden in particular and beeped encouragingly.

"I don't know, Artoo," Padmé said. "It doesn't seem fair to ask for help and not give any details."

The droid made a sound that somehow managed to replicate a shrug, and the image disappeared.

Padmé considered his suggestion. She wasn't asking for help as queen or senator this time. That would have been normal and easy. She was asking for help as *Padmé*, and somehow that made everything messy and complicated. She thought she knew where the boundaries were, but she rarely tested them. She wasn't very good at asking the girls to help her as a friend. They'd spent too much time at work.

But they *were* friends. What she shared with her handmaidens, current and former, was a friendship so deep that it included large parts of her heart. She mourned for Cordé and Versé, even as she rejoiced at the successes the others had found beyond her sphere of influence. Surely she, Padmé, could ask for this.

Decision made, she gathered the fabric so as not to trip on it, stood up, and made her way over to the communications console.

Saché had called her several hours ago, saying she would not be home at a reasonable hour and not to wait up for her. This was, Yané mused, for the best. Their bed was full of sleeping children. A mudslide in one of the eastern regions of Naboo's secondary continent had taken out most of a village four days ago. The only survivors were eight children who had been in a school transport at the time of the disaster. While Saché and the other government representatives worked to stabilize the slide and calculate the full extent of the damages, Yané had opened their house to the children.

Four of them had since been taken in by other family members, but the remaining four, all cousins, seemed to have lost everyone. Yané was doing her best to make them feel safe and welcome, but she knew that trauma was not so easily dealt with. If they wanted to sleep in a pile on the bed she shared with Saché, they were welcome to it. It was plenty big enough.

As she often did when she had a moment to herself, Yané went to her loom. She didn't have a lot of time to make cloth these days, though she still made most of the children's clothing, as well as her own and Saché's. It was always nice to get back to the very beginning of her art form, so she almost decided to ignore the communications console when it chimed for her attention, before common sense reasserted itself. When she saw who was calling, she quivered with excitement.

"Senator!" she said as Padmé appeared in front of her. "To what do I owe the pleasure?"

She knew Padmé was on Naboo, of course. She had arrived after the Geonosis incident and had gone directly to the lake house with a request that she was not to be disturbed. Saché reported that war was spreading, and Naboo was almost certainly going to be involved, but details were few and far between. Still, Yané was pleased to see Padmé.

"Hello, Yané," Padmé said. "I'm sorry to call so late. I hoped you would be available."

"Your timing is perfect," Yané told her. "Saché's still at work, dealing with the mudslide disaster, and all the survivors are asleep in our bed. I'm completely at your disposal."

"Oh," said Padmé. "I'm so sorry. I'd forgotten about the mudslide. Do you have everything you need for additional children? You must be so busy."

"You have plenty of other things to worry about," Yané said. "And so do I, to be perfectly honest, but at the moment, I could use a distraction. What did you want to talk about?"

Padmé hesitated, and in that moment, Yané knew it was a personal favor. If it were work-related, she would have simply stated her reason for calling.

"I would like your advice about a dress," Padmé said finally.

Yané recognized the cloth immediately, or rather, its function if not its particular form. This was going to be a wedding dress. For Padmé. Seemingly out of nowhere, but now that the senator spent so much of her time offworld, it was hardly surprising that she did things Yané was unaware of.

It still hurt, though. Yané let a bit of it show in her face and saw Padmé recognize it for what it was. They didn't need words. This was enough.

"You should use it as your veil," Yané said, getting down to business now that they had cleared the air between them. "A few years ago, the style was to incorporate the fabric into the train or the sash, but I think a veil will be more of a statement piece for you."

Yané's wedding fabric had been incorporated into both the train and the sash, since she used her own fabric and Saché's in the design. Saché's outfit had been the mirror of hers, with wide-legged trousers in place of the skirt to suit her personal taste. That had been almost two years ago.

"That makes sense," Padmé said. "I can handle that much sewing here. Do you have a suggestion for the dress itself?"

Yané looked closely at the cloth in Padmé's hands and then across the floor to where her loom stood. Padmé deserved more than a dress she could cobble together from whatever pieces she had with her. She deserved something made by the hands of a friend. If Yané got out the mechanized ones and drank a whole pot of caf, she could do it. Saché wasn't coming home tonight anyway.

"I'll take care of it," she said.

Padmé's whole face transformed when she smiled. It wasn't the smile of the queen or the senator, but the personal one that Yané saw only infrequently and treasured every time. Whatever Padmé was up to, she was happy, and Yané couldn't deny that Padmé's happiness was one of her very favorite things. That made everything worth it, even the secrets kept as Padmé drifted away from them.

"Thank you," Padmé said. "Thank you so much."

They didn't linger on the channel, even though they both had many things they would have loved to talk about. They had work to do.

Padmé found the sewing bot exactly where she'd hoped to, in one of the workrooms the lake house boasted. It was a house for artists, as most houses in the area were, but this one was specifically set up for the talents of the girls she'd brought here over the years. The lights in the workroom were soft and well-angled, and Padmé immediately got to work.

She wondered briefly what Anakin was up to. She wouldn't see him again until tomorrow afternoon, though he was the only other human in the house. He could sense her, she knew, and he probably felt her excitement and her concerns. She hoped he understood that her feelings were normal. Not everyone had Jedi training in controlling the emotions they projected. He was probably meditating or working on

C-3PO, who still needed to be cleaned before his final plating could be finished. The droid had been on Tatooine, and then Geonosis. His joints were probably full of sand.

The needle flashed as she worked, finishing the edges and modifying the pleats in the veil. It was quiet, and that was strange. Even if no one was talking, the rooms she worked in were always full of people. She was usually surrounded.

The pain of Sabé's absence lanced through her suddenly and with no warning. She missed all of the girls, of course, but Sabé she missed the most. She wasn't even entirely sure where her friend had gone. They hadn't talked about it, what with Padmé running all over the Outer Rim and then the war beginning. There hadn't been time. Sabé had run a variety of offworld missions for Senator Amidala since she'd gone to Coruscant, but Padmé had always given her the time she needed to follow her own interests. Trafficking led to the dark corners of the Republic, and Sabé couldn't always send word. Now, even though this wedding was a secret that must be kept from the galaxy at large, Padmé missed her.

Padmé pushed down the guilt and sadness she was feeling and focused on the good things. She was safe. The Battle of Geonosis had been won, even if the cost had been high. Anakin Skywalker loved her.

And tomorrow she was getting married.

CHAPTER 2

This time it was going to be different. Sabé had decided that years ago, when their first operation on Tatooine had gone sideways. Since then, she hadn't returned to the planet, but she had worked on building up a contact list and identities for both her and Captain Tonra that would allow them to go back and try to liberate people again. Both of them were technically still in the employ of the Naboo senator, but their long-term assignment had not changed. Lacking other orders, Sabé had decided it was time.

Most people in the Outer Rim didn't really care about the escalating Separatist conflict within the Republic. It didn't affect their day-to-day lives, and it didn't involve their governments. They had much more immediate concerns. For those who profited off of pain and suffering, however—the crime lords and the traffickers—any war was an opportunity for more business. Sabé was here to do whatever she could to stop it.

"They're calling it the Clone War," said Tonra, in the copilot's chair.

They'd spent more time away from each other than

together over the past six years. She'd been building her network, and he'd been working much more closely with Typho and Mariek Panaka, protecting the senator. When they did meet up, it was usually for a specific operation that Padmé was running, or because Sabé needed backup. His voice was as reassuring as ever, though, and his presence as solid. Sabé had a lot of doubts about a lot of things these days, but Tonra was never one of them.

"Creative," Sabé said.

"They have to call it something," Tonra said. "Or else how would they sell news holos about it?"

"Two manufactured armies," said Sabé. She shook her head. "I don't like it. Our side has souls. We can't just throw them at mass-produced machines."

"There's significant debate about that," Tonra said. She glared at him, and he held up a hand defensively. "But I agree with you."

Sabé looked at the ship's chronometer. She was still in her bright, fancy-looking clothes and needed to change before they arrived. She looked just fine for a day spent as a high-level aide in the hallowed halls of the Republic Senate or for engaging in important trade negotiations in the Core, but that wasn't who she was anymore. She flipped control of the ship to Tonra's station and made her way to the back compartment.

Technically, a person of her claimed social standing wouldn't have her own craft. They should be taking a public shuttle to Tatooine, if everything was going to be perfect. But Sabé was reluctant to give up the freedom and flexibility that a private ship allowed her, so she had managed to squeeze it into their cover.

Sabon and Arton Dakellen were middling successful traders, specializing in short-haul trips for specific higher-value and low-volume goods. With the onset of the war, they had sold their stake in trading and found land-based jobs that would be more stable during the conflict. Since Sabon owned the ship outright, she got to keep it. The pair were moving to Tatooine, where Sabon would run logistics for a water export company and Arton would maintain the supply chain for one of the local cantinas. Their ship would be generally available for hire, and though it was not to be their primary source of income, it would explain any absences from the planet.

Last time they had come to Tatooine, they had simply shown up. They had asked too many questions. This time, they would be members of the community. It would take longer, and they wouldn't be able to help as directly, but Sabé knew in her heart it was a better plan.

She stripped off her upper-level Coruscant finery but left her undergarments in place. No one would see them, and she was certainly not going to get rid of practical clothing that was going to remain hidden anyway. She pulled a light shirt over her head. It covered her to the wrists, to keep the sun off her skin, but was made of a breathable material. She stepped into sturdy russet-colored trousers. They had plenty of pockets for any tools she would need. Next came the overtunic, a sleeveless vest that fell halfway down her thighs, though slits were cut to the waist so she could move around. It was faded orange in color, giving her a generally dusty appearance. She'd fit right in. Last came a wide belt, where she would carry her purse, canteen, and vibroblade.

She packed the fancy clothes away at the bottom of her trunk, leaving her other Tatooine-appropriate clothes on the top for easy access. They did have an apartment waiting for them, theoretically, but there was no way to tell what the storage would be like. She pulled on her boots and then opened Tonra's trunk. He was perfectly capable of laying out his own clothes, but old habits died hard.

"Your turn," she said, returning to the flight deck and taking her seat.

"We should be dropping out of hyperspace any moment," Tonra said, flipping control back to her.

Sabé prepped their landing permit and docking clearance while Tonra changed. His clothes were mostly the same as hers, only bigger. He wore a blaster openly, an inelegant black-and-gray contraption they'd acquired somewhere. He was settling back into his chair when the comm crackled and a voice came through.

"Freighter One Seventeen, this is port control. State your

business." It wasn't a droid speaking, just an incredibly disinterested person.

"Submitting our permits now," Sabé said, feeding first the landing documents and then their docking permit.

"We read you, Freighter," the voice said. "Bay thirty-one is yours."

"Thank you, Control," Sabé said. The connection had already been cut, but she still had good manners.

"Here we go," Sabé said. She began the landing sequence.

"Again," Tonra added as he went through the copilot's checklist.

Sabé exhaled with a bit of annoyance. They hadn't talked about it, not really, but she knew both of them were still a little sore about how things had turned out the last time they had tried this. They had completely blown their covers and only barely salvaged the operation by using their own funds to buy a shipment of enslaved people. The people had been immediately freed and taken to Karlinus, a planet that welcomed workers and paid them well, but it was hardly the rousing success Sabé had wanted. Nothing rankled like failure and unfinished business.

"I'm glad you could come with me," she said. "I know the guard detail on Coruscant could have used you, and you're probably high-ranking enough to get a regular palace job in Theed if you wanted."

"You don't exactly have to be here, either," Tonra reminded her. "We're both here because we left something undone and we want to try again."

"Now that we're smarter," Sabé added.

"Wiser," Tonra corrected gently. "I'm not sure the galaxy could handle you if you got too much smarter."

Sabé laughed and brought the ship down over Mos Eisley. The city had not improved since the last time she'd seen it. Squat whitish-brown buildings stretched out below them. There was little evidence of public infrastructure. The streets were haphazardly placed and had no fixed width. Wires and water tanks hung everywhere. She knew it wasn't possible, not with the air circulators on the ship, but she felt like she could already smell it: heat and dust and too many people.

Tonra reached over and placed his hand lightly on top of hers. She wasn't alone. They brought the ship in together.

ᘔᘚᘚᘔ

The list Dormé was working from was very short. She wasn't exactly sure how long Padmé was planning to stay on Naboo, and she didn't *want* to know what she was up to, but Dormé had her own task in the meantime. It was a bit morbid, replacing her coworkers, but it had to be done. Cordé and Versé were gone, and Dormé couldn't do everything at once. They needed more handmaidens.

"I think it should be different this time," Padmé had said. Dormé had been on her way back to Theed with Typho. Padmé had already landed and set out for the Lake Country. "When we brought you and the others in, we were looking for specific talents. The first time, I was after look-alikes and friends. I think this time, I am more in need of . . ."

Her voice had trailed off, but Dormé knew where she'd been headed. It wasn't just grief speaking, either. It was practicality.

"You need senatorial aides," Dormé said. "You need handmaidens to actually do what everyone thinks hand-maidens do anyway. They won't be quite as multitalented as your earlier teams, but we can still find people who are loyal and wish to serve."

"Is it fair to ask them to do that?" Padmé said. Service without friendship seemed cold to her. "I offered the rest of you so much more in return, in terms of a relationship with me and a challenge in your work."

"They won't know any other way, Senator," Dormé had said. "And you'll still have me, of course."

"I'll leave it to you, then," Padmé told her. "Thank you."

"My hands are yours," Dormé murmured, and the connection was cut.

Now, sitting with the list of names, Dormé was pleased with how the interviews had gone. The handmaidens were basically legendary. Everyone knew that only the best of the best could be one, no one knew exactly what it was they did, and most people never thought they would ever get the chance to find out. Three of the interviewees were clearly better suited to life in the Theed court itself. Dormé had already sent them a polite rejection and a letter of recommendation to the palace. A fourth was too similar to Dormé in skill set, given what Padmé was looking for now. Even three months ago, zhe would have been perfect. She shared zher name with Saché, in case Saché had need of zher.

This left her with two. She had liked both candidates when she interviewed them and was pleased that they both returned for the secondary talk. They knew they were replacing hand-maidens who had died, and Dormé would not have blamed them if they'd decided to back out.

"The senator is looking forward to meeting you," Dormé told them after they had finished signing their contracts. "Her schedule can be a bit unpredictable, but she's with family at the moment, so you have some time to go home and make your arrangements to leave Naboo. I recommend bringing only a few personal items. We will outfit you with everything else, and it's easier to move quickly."

Both girls nodded and then exchanged glances. Dormé decided to wait them out.

"What about our names?" Elleen asked finally.

Dormé was pleasantly surprised. It wasn't a rule that the handmaidens changed their names, and she hadn't planned to bring it up unless they did, but it was always a good sign. Already, across Naboo, children were being named with the é ending in Padmé's honor. It was a fashion, like the hooded cloaks at court, but it was still part of her legacy.

"We are Naboo," Dormé told them. "I will call you whatever you wish to be called."

"I'll be Ellé then," the girl said. She'd clearly been thinking about it. Dormé looked at the second one.

"Moteé," she said. She wasn't particularly shy; she just preferred to let others talk if they were going to anyway.

"I'll amend the files," Dormé said. "On behalf of Senator Padmé Amidala, I am happy to welcome you."

The new handmaidens left, and Dormé sent their files over to Padmé so she could familiarize herself with them. There was no answer, and Dormé hadn't expected one. As long as she didn't know what Padmé was doing, she couldn't be asked for her opinion of it, and her opinion was nobody's business anyway. Padmé would tell her eventually. That was the way of it.

A soft chime indicated an incoming message. Dormé smiled: it was Typho.

"Are you finished then?" he asked, his holographic face appearing in front of her. She was always glad to see him, even when he was blue and mostly transparent.

"Yes," she said. "A full complement for the trip back to Coruscant."

"Excellent," he said. "I've got a table at that noodle place Eirtaé's been growing algae for. Do you want to go eat art?"

Dormé laughed and told him she'd love to. Her work was important and very fulfilling, but sometimes it was nice to be home.

CHAPTER 3

Saché had come to work fully expecting a long day of debates and discussion as Naboo's legislature worked to deal with the aftermath of the mudslide on the secondary continent. She knew that Yané had the most important part of the situation under control: the survivors were safe and were being taken care of. It was up to everyone else to assess the situation and do their best to make sure nothing like it happened again.

It took a few hours, but the legislature moved at a reasonable pace through their task list. Survey teams were dispatched to the slide site and to the surrounding regions. Engineers were called in to develop new safety mechanisms. Farmers were consulted on how to best move forward with further terracing of the hills. Medical funds were set aside for the orphaned children, to ensure they would be cared for if they needed something beyond what their caretakers could provide. Though their agenda was rooted in disaster, the legislature actually had a pretty good day. They got all their work done, and no one went too badly off topic or tried to manipulate the proceedings for personal gain. In fact, they were about to adjourn for the night when a young legislator from Theed stood up and was granted the floor.

"Honorable colleagues, I know we have had a long day," the young man began. Saché braced herself for the other shoe. "But now that we have dealt with our own crisis on-planet, I feel that we should turn our attention to the galactic situation."

There were some grumblings at that. Everyone knew it was important, but it was late, and they couldn't really do anything until tomorrow anyway.

"I know, my friends," the young man continued. "But we are already here, and a matter of some importance has been brought to my attention, because it affects not just Naboo, but the whole Chommell sector."

That got Saché's attention. Relations with the other Chommell sector planets were cordial, but they had not progressed as nicely as Queen Amidala had hoped they might after her reign.

"In the face of the Clone War," the young man said, trying out the words for what seemed to be the first time, "I turn to the guidance of a military professional to advise the legislature, and yield to Captain Quarsh Panaka."

Now the room buzzed with interest. Quarsh Panaka rarely spoke in public anymore. His calls for further militarization after the ion cannon was built had been almost entirely rebuffed, and most of his credibility with the crown had been spent. He still had friends in the legislature, though, and any time he showed up, it was invariably some sort of event. Saché took advantage of everyone's distraction to make a note to call Yané during the next recess and tell her not to wait up.

Panaka strode to the center of the room. It was an odeon, and small enough that the acoustics worked without the aid of technology. Whatever Panaka said would be heard perfectly clearly, as long as he didn't pace around the floor.

"Legislators," he began, "I'm not interested in keeping you up past your bedtimes for no reason, but with the beginnings of the Clone War, there are things Naboo must deal with."

The murmured response to that was mildly offended, but everyone was too polite to yell at him.

"Appearing on your screens now is a copy of an old bill, once passed in these very halls," Panaka said. Saché looked down at her personal screen and began to read, splitting her focus. "As you'll see, it dates back to the time when Naboo expanded to the uninhabited planets in the sector. As part of their agreement, the colonists signed a contract that remains binding to this day."

"Just tell us what the contract says, Captain." Governor Bibble was clearly on his last nerve.

"Of course, Governor," Panaka said. "In return for Naboo's loan of start-up costs, the colonists agreed to be called upon to supply Naboo in times of emergency. We didn't do it during the Occupation because we didn't have time, but we could have. They would be legally obligated to give us whatever we decided we needed."

Dead silence greeted his statement. Saché leaned on her speaker's button so hard, she thought she might break it.

"Legislator Saché?" the protocol droid recognized her.

"Governor," she said, and stood. "Captain, are the terms of the contract that vague?"

"Yes, I'm afraid they are." He didn't address her by an honorific, and his face softened a little bit when he spoke to her, even as his eyes lingered on the scars he hadn't been able to prevent. After all this time, he *still* didn't fully understand what he'd built. "Once the colonies were economically stable— and they now are—Naboo could call in the loan."

"Do the sector planets know about this?" she asked.

"They do, your honors," he said. Panaka turned away from her to address the general floor again. "We must consider carefully what we do next. War will reach us, in some form or another, soon enough. Naboo has a reputation for providing aid. If we have the Chommell planets to draw upon, as well, this will affect how we approach distribution of resources in the coming days."

"What if they can't support themselves as well as us?" Saché still had the speaker, it seemed, though she wasn't the only person who shouted a variation of the question.

"That's why I brought it to you," Panaka said.

"You have my thanks, Captain," Bibble said. "If you will all take your seats again and return to order, I will take recommendations on how to proceed."

Saché did not bother trying to access the speaker again. Someone else stood to recommend a forty-minute recess for them to read the bill and formulate their thoughts—and grab a snack, or at least that was implied—and Bibble granted it. Saché had nine messages from allies by the time she got to her office, and three from her usual adversaries, all asking what she was going to do. For ten minutes, she ignored everything.

They all remembered the Occupation. They all remembered running out of food and then, because the Trade Federation had ensured it, not being able to distribute the food they had. Most of them had been in camps. But only Saché had been tortured.

The memories of that horrible experience haunted her only infrequently. Usually she would have a nightmare, and then Yané would soothe her back to sleep, and that was all. Sometimes, if mention of the Occupation took her off guard, her breath would catch in her chest and she would remember the pain very clearly. This was neither of those two things. She remembered, but it did not consume her. This was a fire she could channel.

Saché took a deep breath and looked into the mirror she kept in her desk drawer. Rabé had designed two versions of the same makeup for her. One was a cover-up that smoothed her skin to an even tone. She almost never wore it. The second, which she wore almost every day, highlighted the stark difference between her pale skin and the raw redness of her scars. She'd earned them, and they'd hurt *a lot*, so she was going to use them. When she spoke tonight, everyone would see her, and they would know.

Saché returned to the floor thirty minutes later, having contacted her wife and said good night to as many of their children as ran through the transmission. The same chime summoned everyone else. The night stretched on and on as legislators spoke and factions formed. Panaka didn't speak again, but he stayed on the floor the whole time, and Saché wondered how he had found himself with information so vital at this exact time. He wasn't the type to scour old files of Naboo policy for fun. If there was a war, perhaps he was looking for a way back into the Queen's good graces. He did, after all, always have the good of Naboo close to his heart, even if he disagreed with everyone else about how to carry that out.

Finally, Saché's turn to speak arrived, and she rose to address the legislature. She didn't voice any of her speculations, not yet. It was time to find good questions, not spurious ones. And she could always uncover more if no one knew what she was really after.

"My friends, we are at a crossroads," she said. "And we have a choice. We can be dictatorial and ruthless, and ensure our own needs before everyone else's. Or we can cancel the bill outright and declare it water under the bridge. I think you all know where I stand on that."

There was some cheering in the room at her statement.

"What does not change is this," she concluded. "We must reach out to the other planets and see if there is a way we can work together. We all have resources that other planets need, and there is no reason not to cooperate. But it should be done under the auspices of good government, not an outdated bill, signed by our ancestors during desperate times."

It was nearly three in the morning when Bibble called a halt to the proceedings. Saché's speech had been received the most favorably, but there was a larger-than-was-comfortable contingent of legislators who didn't want the bill rescinded at all. They were so worried about hardship befalling them that they couldn't understand—or didn't care—how it would impact others to maintain their standard of living. They could not accept that Naboo might suffer alongside its neighbors, a deliberate choice to join them instead of exploiting them. Their fear made them selfish and shortsighted. So after all of that, there was no vote anyway. Bibble sent them on their way with instructions to return to debate the following day at noon.

Saché thought about trying to catch Panaka on his way out, but he was swamped by the legislators who wanted to keep the bill, and she couldn't stomach talking to any of them, so she went back to her office instead. She sent a message to the governor of Karlinus, an old friend, and to Harli Jafan, who was usually at least a reasonable ally. There was a picture from Yané of a familiar bed filled with children, and a message from Dormé about a person who might make a good assistant. Saché was definitely in need of that, but decided to wait until a more reasonable hour to act on it.

Leaving everything else until after she'd gotten some rest, Saché curled up on the sofa Yané had bought for exactly this purpose and went to sleep.

⟩⩗⩗⟨

Quarsh Panaka's room in the barracks was cold, which was the way he preferred it. Mariek had always turned the heat up, and while he was happy whenever she was happy, this was pretty good, too. The evening in the legislature had gone almost exactly as he had imagined it would: all talk and no resolution. More legislators than he had hoped were actually in favor of keeping the bill as it was. They would be overruled, of course, but there would be concessions and compromises when that happened, and Panaka could use that to strengthen Naboo's defenses.

Before he turned in for the night, he fired off a quick message to Coruscant. Chancellor Palpatine was a busy man, but he still took the time to write to Panaka every once in a while. He said that reading Naboo history and talking about it with friends from home helped him focus and reminded him of his purpose, even as the galaxy turned to war. He would be gratified to know that Panaka had acted on his latest message and that their homeworld would, as always, be as safe as they could keep it.

CHAPTER 4

The sun had risen but not yet cleared the mountains when Padmé dove into the lake. It was her favorite time to go swimming, that moment when there was enough light to see by before the day had truly begun. The water was clear and cold, like always. The lake was fed by mountain streams, and the Naboo took care not to pollute it with agricultural runoff. Before the heat of the day warmed the waters, swimming was an abrupt wake-up. Padmé wanted a clear head.

It wasn't that she felt muddled or unsure of what she was doing. If anything, her conversation with Yané the night before and the meditative hours spent sewing had made her more certain. What troubled her was that she had always thought of herself as a straightforward and honest person. Yes, she kept secrets, but they were for the sake of her planet, her people. And there were always some who knew the whole story. Now her truths were split, divided amongst those she cared about, and none of them had the whole picture. Only she did, alone and at the center of her own life.

She liked it. Even though she ached for her friends and missed her parents and sister, she loved the solitude of this moment, of knowing her decision was hers alone. It was contradictory, something else she'd never been, but she was growing up, and that was bound to change her.

For so long, her life had revolved around other people's perception of her. What she should do and how she should dress. How her decisions would affect masses of people she had never met. It was a tremendous burden, and she'd carried it since she was a child. She hadn't minded—at times she had reveled in the responsibility—but with the freedom of being unknown in front of her, she felt a surge of excitement. Anakin was going to be hers, and she was going to be his, and almost no one in the whole galaxy would share that with them.

Padmé dove down as deep as she could, staying under the water where it was quiet for as long as possible. When her lungs burned for air, she kicked up, breaking the surface with a cascade of water droplets glinting in the morning sun. Everything was perfect. The lake, the house, her spirit. She had built so many things in her life—houses and hospitals, alliances and accords—and now she'd have something that was just for her. Well, just for her and Anakin. They would be something new. And even though they would keep it to themselves, Padmé knew that their love would shine brightly.

The day was starting. She would have to go back to real life eventually. But the lake reminded her, as it always did, of the peace and quiet of home and the promise of places no one else could reach. She kicked toward the pier, refreshed and ready to face the day.

Anakin Skywalker was not entirely ready for this. Which, he realized, was not a surprise. His training had focused entirely on selflessness and detachment. That might be enough for most Jedi, but it was not enough for him.

Truth be told, Anakin had decided to marry Padmé in the kitchen at his stepfather's house. He watched the way Owen and Beru moved around as they prepared lunch, handing each other things before they were asked and laughing when they bumped into each other. It was a connection that had nothing to do with the Force, and Anakin wanted it. His mother must have had something like that with Cliegg, too. It was clear from the way they all spoke of Shmi that she hadn't been an afterthought in the Lars family. She had been the center. And he hadn't been part of it at all.

That wasn't true. They had known who he was the moment they saw him and had immediately taken him into their house. She must have spoken about him frequently and made it clear that if he ever came to visit, he was to be included. And they did include him. Like it was nothing. Like he was family. The Jedi had never given him that. And now he could build his own family.

There was a shrine to Qui-Gon Jinn's memory on Naboo. Ten years had passed, but it was still a popular pilgrimage site. It wasn't the right time of year for memorials, so when Anakin commandeered the house speeder and went out to see it that morning, it was mostly deserted.

Anakin took a seat in the middle of the stone floor and rested his hands on his knees. The metal hand was something he was still adapting to—a protuberance, not yet a true prosthetic. Medically, everything was fine, and from an engineering standpoint, the hand was perfect. Anakin could feel the difference, though, more than the strange sensations that sometimes emanated from knuckles and joints that were no longer there. He already had a list of modifications he was going to make when he got back to the workroom at the Temple. The hand was *his*, and he was going to make sure it was exactly what he wanted.

He shrugged off his worldly concerns and reached out with the Force. He'd heard Qui-Gon's voice in the desert, begging him to listen to his better nature, not to give in to his hatred. He hadn't listened. At the time, he'd told himself he was imagining it, but he knew he was lying. If Qui-Gon was out there, somehow, Anakin owed him an apology. And he would always appreciate the Master's advice.

But he found nothing. Anakin looked deeper. There was so much fighting in his future, but it was all for the good of the Republic, for order. Maybe that was what Qui-Gon wanted him to see. There was always a way for him to make it right.

He felt centered. At peace. Yes, there was a war, and no, he didn't know that much about being married, but he could see the path forward, and he wouldn't have to walk it alone. Looking down at his Jedi robes, he wondered for the first time if he ought to have asked C-3PO to find him a nicer outfit to get married in. He was sure Padmé would have something. Amazing dresses seemed to just happen on Naboo. But no: he was a Jedi getting married. He would at least be true to himself about that. There were enough secrets in his future. He would be married how he wanted to be.

"Thank you, Master," Anakin said, though he didn't know if Qui-Gon had been responsible for anything he'd just seen and felt.

As he prepared to head back to the lake house, his thoughts turned toward Padmé again. He liked it when she was happy, and she had seemed so happy since they arrived back on Naboo. It was a side of her he had never seen before: carefree and casual. Even when they'd come to the lake house before, she had clung to formality like a shield. Now she was entirely relaxed, and they could be absorbed in each other in a way that wouldn't be possible anyplace else.

Anakin strode out of the shrine, a man on a mission. It was his wedding day, and everything was going to be perfect.

Padmé was in no great hurry to do anything, so she stayed in her comfortable robe while her hair dried in the early morning sun. There were several comfortable seats on the lanai for just that purpose, and she was happy to take advantage of them. She did have a list of things to do, but she had plenty of time. As she watched the sun grow brighter on the surface of the lake, she heard the low hum of an approaching craft. Anakin had taken the speeder that morning, so she didn't give it much thought until the craft came into view.

Even at a distance, Padmé could recognize a royal Naboo vessel. This one was for small traveling groups, something the Queen might use for a quick escape from the city or to send members of her circle on an official mission. It could only be headed for the lake house, Padmé knew. There were no other houses in the area where the skiff could dock. She secured her robe and coiled her damp hair into a low knot at the back of her head before making her way down to the pier.

Queen Jamillia disembarked alone, leaving her guards and handmaidens behind so she could talk to Padmé privately. She was dressed in heavy, dark red velvet, but her face was bare, and she didn't have an elaborate headpiece over her hair. Whatever the subject of her visit, it wasn't precisely formal.

"Your Majesty," Padmé said, inclining her head. "To what do I owe the honor?"

"Senator," Jamillia said, "I apologize for intruding on you while you're healing. You are well?"

"Still a bit sore," Padmé admitted. "But no complaints beyond that. Will you come up to the lanai with me? I haven't had breakfast yet."

"I can't stay that long," Jamillia said. "I have a favor to ask of you, if you're willing to listen. It's a bit sensitive, which is why I would need you to handle it unofficially."

It never occurred to Padmé to refuse her. She knew Anakin would understand. He, too, served a purpose greater than himself.

"I am happy to do what I can," Padmé said. "Please, tell me what you need."

"Several members of the Torada Collective were off-planet when the war broke out," Jamillia said. "That's not unusual, of course, but five of them in particular are behind Separatist lines, and their parents would like them retrieved."

The Torada Collective was an assortment of Naboo artists who didn't fit in particularly well with their peers. Some wanted more wealth and recognition than they could get from Naboo's art communities, some had political ideals that weren't represented in the legislature, and some just wanted to rebel against their families' wishes. They had a few compounds on the planet where they could live and work in peace, but many chose to travel frequently.

"Are they all together?" Padmé asked.

"Yes," Jamillia said. "I can send you the coordinates. It's possible that they aren't in any danger yet, but I would like to be as prepared as possible. I know you had a Jedi escort back to Naboo, and I can't send my own security officers to do this. There are Naboo all over the galaxy, and I can't be seen to favor this group."

"Of course," Padmé said. She knew there was something Jamillia wasn't saying, some reason the Queen was desperate enough to come to Padmé instead of using official channels. But Padmé also knew when to not ask questions. She had been in politics for a long time, and Jamillia was a person she trusted. "I can take a small team and have them back safely in time for dinner."

It was a bit optimistic, but she and Anakin had planned a sunset ceremony anyway. People's lives were more important.

"Thank you, Senator," Jamillia said. "If you'll excuse me, I must return to the capital."

"Travel well, Your Majesty," Padmé said.

"You as well, Senator," Jamillia replied.

The Queen walked back onto the royal skiff, and it took off immediately. The vessel disappeared in moments, leaving only ripples on the lake's surface to mark its path. Padmé felt like she had dreamed the whole thing, except that she had a datachip from the Queen, marked priority one, with all the details she was going to need for the journey.

Another hum became audible in the early morning air, and Padmé saw Anakin returning across the lake in his speeder. C-3PO was determined to keep them apart before the ceremony, but there was no way Padmé was going to undertake this mission without Anakin's help. There were no other guards to take with her, for one thing, and more important, she was thrilled at the idea of working with him again. She watched as he docked the speeder and leapt gracefully onto the pier in front of her.

"What is it?" he asked. "I sensed something unexpected."

"We have to take a quick trip," she told him, a smile playing on her lips. His mouth twitched in response. "A bit of heroics, and then back here for the wedding."

"I'll break the news to Threepio while you get dressed," Anakin said.

He offered her his arm, and they walked into the house together.

CHAPTER 5

Nooroyo stretched out below them, a biodiverse planet of lush jungles and rocky beaches. They were headed for the warmest part of the world, which was fortunate because the only adventurous gear Padmé had on hand at the lake house was a new version of her shredded whites from the Geonosis arena, and those were designed for hot climates. Anakin wore his tunic and tabard but left his cloak hanging in a compartment aboard the ship.

Padmé loved the expression on his face when he saw a new planet for the first time. Even Geonosis, which hadn't exactly been a pleasure trip, had softened his eyes and erased some of the stress from his shoulders. Nooroyo, green and beautiful, lit his eyes with a boyish inquisitiveness and irrepressible delight. She was happy to give him the moment.

A voice cut through the quiet: "Unidentified vessel, this is Nooroyo primary landing control. Please identify yourself immediately."

"Hello, Control, we are a Naboo civilian ship here to see some of our artists. They live in a settlement north of Nooro-City," Padmé said.

There was a pause, and Padmé suspected they were scanning the ship. Her senatorial ship was unarmed, and they had not come with an escort of fighters. If they ran into trouble, Anakin's piloting would have to be enough to get them out of it.

"Situation confirmed," said the voice. "Please follow the assigned flight path and landing designation. All ships are registered."

"That's new," Padmé said after the channel was closed. "Nooroyo is even more welcoming than Karlinus, back in the Chommell sector. They don't usually register ships."

"We probably have our Separatist friends to thank for that," Anakin said. "I don't like all this sneaking around instead of just saying the real reason we're here, but it's probably safer for everyone if we can get this over with quickly."

Padmé nodded her agreement and flew the ship along the prescribed route to the artist commune. Anakin, for all his gruffness about the Separatists, spent the entire time staring out the viewport at new plants and rock formations. She landed the ship in the designated dock, setting down as lightly as she could so as not to disturb the local flora.

The artist commune was a well-kept collection of buildings on the bank of a wide, rushing river. The buildings were all painted bright blue, and flowers were everywhere, gardens lining the walkways and filling nearly every available space inside the sculpted metal fence. The smell was amazing as

Padmé exited the ship, a warm breeze wafting away the stale air of space and replacing it with the freshness of new growth. R2-D2 beeped appreciatively.

A tall human woman walked toward them. She didn't look like she was in a hurry. Padmé couldn't tell if she was one of the Naboo they'd been sent to rescue, but there would be time for that after introductions.

"Greetings, travelers," the woman said. "My name is Celena, and this is my property. You are welcome here, as long as you abide by our rules. Have you come to stay long?"

"Hello," Padmé said. "We haven't come to stay long at all, though your home is so beautiful, I wish we had more time. We're here on behalf of the Queen of Naboo. Some of her people are here, and she wanted to be sure they were safe, given recent events."

Celena's face stiffened, her porcelain skin tightening around her eyes as she blinked slowly.

"That is understandable," she said. "We are all galactic citizens, regardless of our political affiliations."

Her eyes landed on Anakin, taking in his distinctive clothing and hairstyle, but she said nothing to draw attention to it.

"Come," she said. "I will take you to see those you seek."

"Thank you," murmured Padmé. Anakin told R2-D2 to remain with the ship, and they set out along the neatly manicured pathway.

"We welcome everyone, here," Celena said as they walked.

It seemed to be her standard pitch. "Anyone who wishes to make art without oversight may stay."

"You mentioned rules?" Anakin said. "What sort of things do the people who stay here have to do?"

"We're anti-violence, so conflict is not permitted," Celena said. "Any disputes must be settled by me. Residents can't be unreasonably messy in their quarters, and they must help maintain the gardens and such while they stay here."

"That seems more than fair," Anakin said approvingly.

"There are other rules about food and the like, but that won't be relevant to you if you're not going to stay," Celena said.

It was an invitation to stop asking questions, and Padmé was gracious enough to take it.

They walked under a long archway threaded with vibrantly colored flowers, and Celena paused at the end of it.

"If you will wait here," she said. She didn't wait for an answer before heading to one of the little blue houses.

Padmé turned her face toward the arbor and breathed deeply. The flowers smelled as colorful as they looked, and it had been a while since she had been in such a beautiful garden.

"Do you think your father would show me how to make this sort of flower . . . thing?" Anakin asked. "When we visited him, I noticed his garden and how much you liked it. I know we can't do anything like that right now, but maybe someday?"

"The hard part is getting him to stop," Padmé said. She smiled at the thought of Anakin building her a garden, of him learning Naboo woodworking customs in the same way she had when she was growing up.

"I'll add it to our list," Anakin said.

"It's a very long list," Padmé said. She couldn't help sounding a little resentful when she said it.

"But it's ours," Anakin said. He picked a fallen blossom off the ground and tucked it behind her ear, grinning when she smiled at him.

Their quiet moment was ended by the muffled sound of raised voices within the house. It was impossible to make out the words, but at least one person was clearly pretty angry about something. After a few more moments, Celena emerged with a young human male behind her. He was dressed in Naboo clothes, wide-shouldered and spattered with brightly colored paint. He had a pair of exoskeletal braces on his legs and walked leaning on two canes. Celena went back into the house.

"There are supposed to be five of them," Anakin said quietly.

"We've got to start somewhere," Padmé said. She turned toward the young man. "Hello. My name is Padmé. The Queen asked me to come here and make sure you were all okay."

"My name is Kharl, and I know why you're here," he said.

"Jamillia wants to tell our parents we're safe at home. I have to tell you, it's going to be a hard sell. The others really don't want to go back."

"But it could be dangerous here." Anakin leaned forward. "Naboo is your home."

"This is our home." Kharl threw his arms wide to include the whole compound. Padmé could hardly blame him. It was wonderful, even if war was closing in.

"Kharl, we know you've chosen to live here, and we respect that," Padmé said. "But Queen Jamillia can't protect you here. Your parents can't protect you here. We just want you to be safe."

Kharl blinked slowly at them, his eyes going glassy for a moment before he cleared them. It was enough for Anakin.

"You're on spice!" he said, a weighted load of accusations behind his words. "Is that why you won't go back to Naboo? Because you need to keep getting your fix?"

"I take the medical-grade stuff," Kharl said coldly. All signs of welcome friendliness disappeared from him. "I have a chronic condition that causes me immense pain. Spice makes it tolerable. I can't get it on Naboo, because of the laws there. I can barely function when I'm at home, and on Nooroyo, I can do my work."

Naboo's medical system was good, but it wasn't perfect. There were some things that couldn't be cured. Doctors argued over the best treatments while their patients waited, desperate for relief. Spice was generally frowned upon, dismissed as a recreational high that caused more damage than it solved, but its abilities to numb pain were undeniable.

"Is everyone here for spice?" Padmé asked as gently as she could. She didn't want to judge, but she had to know.

"No," Kharl said. "But the Separatists certainly are. And they don't want it for pain management."

Padmé pinched the bridge of her nose. This was much more complicated than she'd been led to expect. She couldn't fault Jamillia, though. It was probable that no one on Naboo fully understood the reason these artists had chosen Nooroyo as their home.

"Our task is to bring you all back to Naboo," Padmé said. "I can understand that you are reluctant, but if the Separatists are here for spice, it's only a matter of time before this planet is swamped with fighting. It won't just be the droids and the Republic, either. Criminals will get involved. We can't force you to do anything, but I would appreciate it if you would make our case to your friends."

Kharl gave it a few moments of thought and then nodded reluctantly.

"It'll be a hard sell," he said again. "Most of us left Naboo for a reason, even if the reasons aren't all the same."

"I've seen a lot of terrible places," Anakin said. "Naboo is a good one."

"I know," Kharl said. "It's so good that sometimes it forgets that not everyone in the galaxy has it so easy. Most of us are here because we don't want to forget."

Anakin narrowed his eyes as he absorbed Kharl's declaration, but he didn't say anything.

"You're exactly the kind of person we need on Naboo," Padmé told the young man. "Working for change, not letting us become complacent. But it's not the kind of work everyone wants to do."

"I just want to paint," Kharl agreed. "The idea of public speaking makes me want to vomit. I do like teaching though. There are kids here, and I teach them about making paint colors and preserving plants."

Padmé smiled, soaking in the sun. Kharl looked closely at her for a moment, and then all the color drained from his face.

"What is it?" Anakin said, instantly detecting the emotional shift.

"You're not just a representative of the Queen," Kharl said, horrified. "You're Amidala."

"Yes," Padmé said. She hadn't expected to be recognized, but there was no point in denying it.

"You can't be here," Kharl said. "You cannot be here."

His alarm was coming off of him in waves. It was obvious, even without the Force. Anakin grabbed Padmé's arm, ready to drag her back to the ship. She shook him off.

"Why not?" Padmé asked.

"Gunray is here," Kharl hissed. "In person. For the spice negotiations. Your ship will have been tagged. He might not recognize it as yours, but he'll definitely recognize it as Naboo and send someone to check. You have to go. Now."

Anakin grabbed her arm again, and this time Padmé didn't fight him. Nute Gunray had evaded justice so many times, and now he was unreachable by Republic authority. And he was *here*. Gunray had watched her fight to the death and cheered when she was wounded. Padmé was not a violent person, or a vengeful one, but for a brief moment she understood entirely what Anakin had felt when he stood in that Tusken village on Tatooine.

"Tell the others," Padmé barked as Anakin pulled her back toward the ship. "If they want to come, they come now. I will make sure Queen Jamillia understands the situation when they get home. We'll set you up somewhere isolated, if you want. Just talk to them."

Kharl nodded and began to make his way back to the house. Padmé stopped resisting Anakin's direction and followed him back along the path to the ship. The flowers still filled the air with their glorious scent. The Trade Federation couldn't ruin everything.

CHAPTER 6

"This really isn't how I thought this day would go," Anakin said. He was in the pilot's chair, prepping to leave. He never presumed on board Padmé's ship, but they both realized this was an exception. "I thought our biggest problem was going to be dealing with Artoo getting overexcited about flowers or something."

"I want to tell you that it's probably not an omen," Padmé replied. She did her half of the preflight checks as quickly as possible. Behind her, she heard R2-D2 whirring as he reinforced the shields. "But I'm pretty sure things like this are going to keep happening."

Outside, a droid starfighter buzzed close to the collection of houses. It hovered between the commune and their ship.

"Attention, Nooroyo residents," it said. "An offworld vessel has been logged at this location. Please wait for inspection team to arrive."

"There's no use trying to destroy it," Anakin said. "It will have already registered the location and sent a message back."

"Agreed," Padmé said. "We just have to be ready to go as soon as possible."

"We can't wait for them to decide," Anakin said. "Good reason or no, Kharl is a spice user, and the rest of them are probably troublemakers, too. If they don't want to leave, they deserve whatever they get."

"I will not abandon people to the Separatists if I can possibly help them," Padmé said.

"You're going to have to start looking at the big picture in this war, Padmé." Anakin looked unusually calm when he said the words, like he was drawing on the Force to stabilize himself. "There are going to be losses."

"And I will fight every one," Padmé told him.

Anakin sighed, but didn't press the point any further. The engines hummed as the control board indicated they could take off whenever they wanted to. Through the viewport, Padmé could see two figures approaching the ship, and went back to the ramp to meet them.

Kharl wasn't carrying any luggage, and neither did he seem to have a device that did it for him. The girl beside him had two large packs and an instrument case. She had brown skin and long dark hair. Padmé was one of few people who had seen Queen Jamillia without makeup, and the resemblance was unmistakable. Jamillia's urgency became clear, as did her need to maintain discretion. A mission to save one person was a risky political move, but a completely understandable personal one. Rescuing the Queen's sister, even with the election looming and Jamillia on her way out of power, was important.

"This is Antraya," Kharl said. "She's ready to go."

Padmé stood aside so Antraya could get on board. She could tell the Queen's sister was unhappy about leaving Nooroyo and her friends there. She was doing it for Jamillia, which was something else Padmé could understand.

"I can't promise another chance will come for the rest of you," Padmé said. "This might be your only way of getting back to Naboo."

"We know," Kharl said. "We didn't have a lot of time to talk about it, obviously, but we all know what we're getting into. And it's important you leave before the scanning team gets here."

"Will that cause trouble for the rest of you?" Padmé asked.

"We'll be fine," Kharl said. "We're not at home on Naboo anymore, but it's still where we're from. It's not perfect, but it's a good place. It's just not for us. Maybe, out here, we'll be able to make the rest of the galaxy a little bit more like it."

"May the Force be with you," Padmé said. The engines flared, and she knew that Anakin was anxious to leave.

"Go!" Kharl said.

Padmé ran up the ramp and closed the door. As soon as the seal was in place, Anakin brought the ship up, and by the time Padmé and Antraya had made it to the flight deck, they were in the upper atmosphere.

"We're being scanned," Anakin said, his fingers flying

across the control panel. "But they're not going to catch up before we jump."

"I appreciate you doing this for my sister," Antraya said. "Even though it's not the way I would have chosen."

"I know," Padmé said. "And I'm sorry you have to make this sacrifice."

Anakin got the ship clear of the planet and away from the moons, finished the calculations, and made the jump to hyperspace. As soon as space was streaking steadily past the viewport, he blew out a lungful of air and sat back in the pilot's seat.

"I can't believe we didn't have to fight anyone," he said.

"I'm glad we didn't," Padmé said.

"I don't like not being able to control the outcome," Anakin said. "There was nothing I could do to help."

"That's why you take *me* on missions," Padmé said. She forgot they had company and said it more flirtatiously than she should have.

"Who are you people anyway?" Antraya asked.

"Friends of the Queen," Padmé said, and explained no further.

Antraya, apparently no more comfortable with politics than Anakin was, huffed dismissively and slumped down in her chair. She'd left her big packs in the hold but cradled the instrument case protectively against her chest. Padmé didn't know what she played, but clearly it meant a lot to her.

"We'll have you home soon," Anakin told her.

"What's the rush?" Antraya asked. "Have you got plans?"

"Something like that," Padmé said. She couldn't help laughing at her own words.

$$\text{ʒ\kern-0.1em ∨\kern-0.1em ∨\kern-0.1em ʅ}$$

Anakin didn't disembark from the senatorial ship while Padmé delivered Antraya to the Queen. Very few people knew he was on Naboo, and he was happy to keep it that way. He watched through the viewport as Padmé spoke briefly to Jamillia, and then the two sisters embraced. Antraya might have been reluctant to come back to Naboo, but there was no reluctance in how she felt about her sister. Anakin wondered how Obi-Wan was doing. They didn't often spend long periods of time apart.

Padmé disappeared from the viewport and Anakin could hear her making her way back to the flight deck through the ship. It was a quick flight back to the lake house, and they still had about two hours before the sun set, but he knew Padmé would probably need that much time to change, since there was no one to help her. Still, there were a few things he wanted to talk to her about, so he set a somewhat circuitous route back to the house.

"I'm sorry for being so abrupt while we were back on Nooroyo," he said when she sat down next to him. She reached out and took his hand, weaving her fingers with his metal ones as though nothing had changed.

"It's all right," she said. "Even Jedi have adrenaline."

"It's not just that." He raised her fingers to his lips. "We're both trained differently to do a similar job, and both of those jobs are different now, because of the war. I should be more patient with you while you adjust. I know you'd be patient with me, if the situation was reversed."

"Are you worried about taking command of troops?" Padmé asked. "I know we both did it on Geonosis, but that was different. This is going to be long-term."

"I wouldn't say I'm worried," Anakin said. "I'm concerned about how the Jedi will react to having an army, but I know that I can handle it. It'll be nice to go into battle with more people, not just me and Obi-Wan."

The ship slid through Naboo's lower atmosphere, rainbows dancing on the silver hull as condensation clung to the paneling.

"Will you tell him?" Padmé asked.

"No," Anakin said. "He wouldn't understand. None of them would."

"I'm sorry," she said. "I know that concealing things doesn't come naturally to you."

"Well, I have the best teacher," he said. He was trying to sound lighthearted about it, but it didn't quite land.

Behind them, R2-D2 chirruped.

"Threepio sent how many messages?" Anakin asked. "And you screened all of them?"

Padmé laughed as the first of several messages from their anxious protocol droid began to play in front of her.

"We have plenty of time," she said. "I'm sure that's what Artoo has been telling him."

R2-D2 beeped affirmatively as the lake house came into view below them. Anakin was smiling as he brought the ship down, looking at her like she was a planet he was seeing for the first time.

CHAPTER 7

The Clone War had begun. It was undeniable, and even though no one really seemed to know exactly what that meant, the war had come at last to Padmé Amidala's little bubble of tranquility in the lake house on Naboo. C-3PO wasn't the only person who had sent her a number of messages while she was on Nooroyo. Bail's steady stream of updates hadn't slowed, and even Mon Mothma had sent a few short comms her way. Still, she would hold on to her peace for a little bit longer, because she wanted to. Padmé closed the messages Bail had been sending her without responding to any of them. It was almost sunset and it was her wedding day.

Padmé had only worked with the clone troopers briefly on Geonosis. Emotions were high, and she'd been running on adrenaline, so it wasn't until afterward that she'd had time to think about it. The troopers had looked to her for orders and followed them when she spoke. They had been polite and concerned about her physical well-being. They hadn't questioned her. It was almost like the teams Padmé was used to working with, but not quite.

It had been easy. And that terrified her.

Padmé had never been one for spontaneous decisions. She planned. She anticipated outcomes and the consequences they would bring. She didn't always share her thought process, of course, but she had one, and even her most reckless decisions were considered. That had served her well professionally for more than a decade, since before her election as Queen of Naboo. To be perfectly honest, she was a little bit tired of living for other people, of always considering others before herself. She wanted something that was *hers*. Surely she could manage both at the same time.

It had been easy to fall for Anakin Skywalker. And that terrified her, too.

She had thought herself immune to such matters. Yes, she'd had adolescent crushes, and yes, there were people she found attractive, but none of that had ever gotten into her head the way Anakin did. She'd always been able to move past it, quickly, avoiding entanglements and returning to work. She'd tried to do the same thing when she realized what her feelings for Anakin were leading toward, and she had almost succeeded, but in the face of death, she had decided to throw caution to the wind.

And that was love, wasn't it? It wasn't like there was anyone she could ask.

The secrecy didn't bother her. She'd kept secrets all her life. This one was Anakin's, primarily, because he stood to lose the most if they were exposed, but she was happy to be a part of it.

C-3PO, newly golden, bustled into the room, breaking her out of her reverie. The droid was officious and strange—she couldn't help wondering how his programming had ended up on Tatooine for Anakin to scavenge—but he was efficient. Once she and Anakin had decided to have an actual wedding, the droid had sprung into action, insisting on all manner of ancient Naboo and Tatooine customs. Padmé would have protested, but Anakin genuinely seemed to enjoy the attention the droid was paying him, so she let C-3PO do all the organizing. They had the rest of their lives.

"It is time to get dressed, my lady," C-3PO said. "Artoo tells me you usually have help for this portion of formal events, and since you do not, I have done what I can to organize your dressing room to make everything as accessible as possible."

"Thank you, Threepio," Padmé said.

"Do you need me for anything?" the droid asked awkwardly. "I'm afraid my programming does not include personal grooming, but I could hold something for you, I suppose?"

An image of the protocol droid trying to braid her hair flashed through Padmé's mind, and she did her best not to laugh. C-3PO took himself very seriously, and the offer had been made in good faith.

"I'll be all right, Threepio," she said. "Is Anakin looking well?"

The droid clucked at her.

"You will not get anything out of me, my lady!" he said. "But it does not appear that anything will impede my schedule, if that is an acceptable answer."

He walked stiffly out of the room, a characteristic of his construction, not his demeanor, and Padmé allowed herself a smile when he left. The protocol droid must have been an absolute hit with the moisture vaporators back at the Lars homestead. She was glad Anakin had brought him when they left Tatooine. In addition to being the last thing that connected Anakin to his mother and homeworld, he was also quickly becoming indispensable. Padmé had never had particularly good luck with protocol droids, but perhaps this one, built by a little boy who wanted to help his mother, was exactly the sort of droid the galaxy needed.

The dress from Yané was already spread out on her bed. It had arrived at lunch, and Threepio had unpacked it immediately because he didn't want it to wrinkle. Looking at it, Padmé had no idea how Yané had managed such exquisite work so quickly, even with the help of her mechanical looms. The dress was a perfect match for the fabric Padmé had turned into her veil, and it was absolutely gorgeous, besides. Elegant draping and myriad seed pearls were only the beginning. The lacework and embroidery nearly took Padmé's breath away. It was beautiful.

She'd already decided on simple makeup and hair, even before C-3PO reminded her that she would have to do it herself. She wasn't getting married as a senator or representing the planet of Naboo. This was just for her and for Anakin. The veil would cover most of her head anyway, and between the dress, the lake, and what was shaping up to be a perfect Naboo sunset, she was more than certain she would look just fine.

She got to work quickly, twisting her hair into simple coils that would hold all the pins from her veil. Then she did her face, making sure to highlight her features instead of mute them, as she usually did. When that was done and set, she put on her shift and underdress. Too late, she realized that the dress from Yané buttoned up the back—about a million tiny pearl buttons she couldn't possibly reach on her own.

For a moment, her loneliness threatened to crush her. Her friends were all far away. She didn't even know where Sabé was. Her parents didn't know she was on the planet. Her colleagues in the Senate knew only the generalities of where she'd gone when she disappeared after Geonosis.

But Anakin was here.

She reminded herself that she'd chosen this. She wanted this. She was doing this, not for her planet or her people, but for her heart. She was going to get into this dress. And then she was going to get married.

⁊�⍟⍦

As far as Anakin was concerned, everything was perfect. C-3PO had finally been convinced that his preparations were sufficient and was standing off to the side with R2-D2. The officiant, a man Anakin had met only a few moments ago but who seemed pleasant enough, was complimenting the droid on a particular flower arrangement that Anakin hadn't even really noticed. He had eyes only for the lake and the sky, and for Padmé.

When she came out onto the lanai, he felt like he was in an airlock that had been vented. His whole world closed in around his vision of her, pale and perfect in the setting sun. The veil that covered her hair was beyond intricate, and its delicate weavings spilled into her train, carrying what seemed like entire constellations of stars, shimmering in the light. She was always the most beautiful thing he'd ever seen, but right now she defied description.

At first, he barely heard the words the officiant said, binding them together for legal and spiritual purposes. The Jedi had no marriage words, of course, but the Naboo did, and as Anakin's attention widened from Padmé's presence to the speaker beside them, he listened and inscribed the words on his heart.

When the officiant stepped away, Anakin reached for Padmé with his left hand. After a moment of hesitation—a hesitation she did not share—he reached out with his right hand, as well. She stepped close, her face turned up to his. She was so solemn now, but he could feel the joy of her bubbling underneath the surface. This is how it would be with them. One face to the public and one face to each other. He would take it. He would relish it.

Anakin Skywalker bent his head and kissed his wife.

CHAPTER 8

The Jedi Council dispersed quickly, but Master Yoda stayed in his chair. Already, his compatriots were shipping out across the galaxy with the army they had somehow acquired, responding to Separatist threats in every corner of the Republic. Four of them had been part of the meeting via hologram, and Yoda knew that number would only rise in the days to come. Even he would go out, eventually. He had seen it.

But for now, he would remain. On Coruscant, yes. In the Temple, assuredly. In this chair, for as long as possible. Old he might be, but his stubbornness showed itself from time to time, and from time to time he indulged it.

Around him, the great city-planet thrummed with life. Some Jedi found Coruscant cold and sterile, but Yoda never had any trouble following the Force connections among the countless beings who lived there. There was very little of the reliable pulse of nature, but the crush of sentient beings going about their days more than made up for it. Sometimes Yoda found it too noisy and turned within himself, but tonight he wanted to feel the whole city at the same time.

The council room windows were wide, and the lights of Coruscant gleamed. There were the steady lines of the Senate building and the various other tall buildings that breached the planet's uppermost levels. There were also the moving lines of traffic, weaving a net through each community and occasionally spiraling down toward the city's lower levels. Everything was linked here, just as much as it was in the lushness of the Felucian jungles, and Yoda could feel it all.

He missed the days when the Order had let him take younglings out on adventures, beyond just the usual quest for their kyber crystals. He had enjoyed the travel, the company of young minds, and the way they had all moved around him in the Force. It was dangerous now, and he was old, but he still wished for those simpler times.

He shook his head. No good would come from distraction, or from dwelling in the past. He would eventually turn to meditation before he left the room for the night, but before that, he had a job to do. He reached over to his armrest and entered a call into his holoprojector.

"Master Yoda?" came the voice of Bail Organa as the senator flickered into view before him. "What can I help you with this evening?"

Bail Organa was one of the best allies the Jedi had in the Senate. They had worked with him the most, and his faction of loyalists was highly respected. If there was a mission of stealth that needed to be carried out, Organa was the one to set it up.

He was very reluctant to participate in the war, though he had not held back any of Alderaan's considerable resources and was at the forefront of organizing most relief, aid, and resupply efforts. Yoda found that particularly reassuring.

"A strange lead have we, Senator," Yoda said. "To your interest it might be."

The senator raised his eyebrows.

"Is this about that resupply company we red-flagged?" Bail asked. "We didn't find anything during our investigation, but we didn't have time to be too precise."

"It is," Yoda told him. "Very suspicious, one of the companies is. Very suspicious of us! Demanded a contact, they have, but no Jedi will they see. Only a senator, sent in secret."

That part had made Mace Windu as close to infuriated as the man ever got. It was the opposite of the way it should have been. The *Jedi* were the trustworthy ones. The Senate was always wildly unpredictable, especially with delicate missions like this.

"That's going to be difficult to arrange," Bail said. "My faction is nearly run off their feet trying to hold the loyalists together. If one of them disappeared, it would definitely not go unnoticed."

"Yes, yes," Yoda said. "Always in motion the Senate is, but especially when the Senate is at war. More thought, I will give this, and so will you, I think."

"Thank you, Master Yoda," Bail said. He looked tired.

"Your information is always appreciated, even if it takes us some time to act on it."

Yoda disconnected the call and turned his attention back to the cityscape before him. As he closed his eyes and reached out with the Force, he thought again of children and of new things, and of finding paths of light through the dark.

Bail Organa pinched the bridge of his nose and then rubbed his face. He'd been awake for what felt like hours, trying to wade through the full policies of what the Chancellor was now entitled to do and keep up with the new policies his faction was hoping to pass. His aides were just as busy, reading other documents and news updates and distilling things down for him, even though his brain already felt like it was about to explode. He knew Mon Mothma was still in her office, doing the same thing he was. He had no idea where Padmé Amidala had gone, and he didn't know when she'd return. He kept her updated, nonetheless. She'd been injured on Geonosis and deserved some recovery time, but he needed her back rather badly.

In the guest chair, well out of the line of traffic, sat Representative Binks. Jar Jar had worked in the Senate for more than half a decade now, and he was excellent at organizing files and remembering what people had said in random conversations, but his naiveté had not faded. The Gungan's well-meant speech in the Senate had allowed the Chancellor powers that Bail did not approve of, but he was enough of a realist to admit that it would have happened anyway. Chancellor Palpatine had a way of getting what he wanted, but having it come from his faction smarted a little bit and put Bail on the back foot as he tried to move forward. At least the Chancellor owed them a favor now, and not someone else.

The new information from Master Yoda was too good to pass up. There was a resupply company that someone on Alderaan had subcontracted with—normal enough, especially with the galaxy mobilizing on this scale—but the company was decidedly strange. Bail's people had looked into it as much as they could, as had his wife's, but they were all swamped. This new tip, given to the Jedi but still insistent on senatorial involvement, was the only lead they had. Bail just had to figure out where on his list of priorities it went.

A cup of caf appeared on his desk, a small bit sloshing over the side as Jar Jar set it down.

"Whoops," said the Gungan.

"It's all right," Bail said, mopping up the mess himself. "I appreciate it."

"Yousa needing sleep, not caf," Jar Jar said.

"You're absolutely correct, my friend," Bail said. Then he downed most of the cup in one gulp, even though it was quite hot. "Unfortunately, I think I'm more likely to get caf."

"Everyone is doing their job, working hard," Jar Jar said. He tapped his long nose. "What weesa needing is someone who is being in two places at the same time."

Bail blinked. Jar Jar went back to his chair and tried to stay out of the way. He knocked over a stack of datapads, clucked at himself, and began to reorganize them. Bail mostly forgave him.

"Thank you, Representative Binks," Bail said. "That is exactly the kind of solution I was hoping to find."

He sent another message to Senator Amidala. Nothing specific, of course, but a very cryptic suggestion that she return to Coruscant as soon as she was able. He had the commissary send up enough dinner for everyone on his staff, and a few of the aquatic delicacies he knew Jar Jar liked. Thus fortified, he plowed back into the documents that outlined the Chancellor's new powers, and tried to imagine how he was ever going to work around him.

⟋⎵⎴⎵⟍

Sometimes, in his simpler fantasies, Chancellor Palpatine imagined burning the Senate to the ground. It was petty and foolish, and wouldn't really solve any of his problems, but he liked the idea of everyone running around screaming in fear and confusion while he got to watch. What was happening now was almost as satisfying, if somewhat less immediately destructive. The Senate was grappling with their new army and his new powers, trying to find out where they could press advantages as individuals and as factions, and still attempting to run the day-to-day operations of the Republic. If he waited long enough, they might light the building for him.

Palpatine enjoyed the rush that came with manipulating people. It had been one of his greatest skills since he was a boy, and he had honed it to a blade so sharp, people rarely even noticed he'd cut them with it until they'd lost too much blood. No Jedi-sanctioned cauterization for the wounds he chose to inflict. They bled, and they spread infection in ways that sometimes surprised—but always delighted—him. It was his favorite way of expanding his own power, the only way that was safe with so many Jedi close by. He had other options, of course, things he'd learned as a young man out in the galaxy, but those he kept close to his chest.

He could draw on them in quiet ways, though. Right now, for instance, he could sense the feelings of any number of senators and their staffs as they scurried around the building, responding to the new threats of war. This was when he felt the most supreme. Not when he acted on his rage, but when he pooled it, used it as a focus to grow. There were powers in the galaxy he had no access to, and that galled him, but he had this, and it made him strong.

Mas Amedda came into the room, drawing Palpatine's attention from the flurry of emotions that were running through the floors below.

"What is it?" he asked.

"The Jedi Skywalker is on Naboo," Amedda told him. "Kenobi returned with the others, but Skywalker is not with them."

The boy hadn't gone to Naboo for the weather. That much was obvious.

"Make sure he comes to see me when he returns," Palpatine instructed. "Not immediately, of course. He can go to the Temple first. But I want to talk to him before they ship him out somewhere."

"I'll make sure of it," Amedda said. "Do you need anything else?"

The list of things that Palpatine needed was long and incredibly secret. Mas Amedda had a general idea what his chancellor was up to, but Palpatine didn't burden him with details. He had ways of keeping his aides under his control. The Chagrian was very useful when it came to dealing with politicians Palpatine didn't have time to talk to, and losing him would be deeply inconvenient.

"No, thank you," he said. It was his only dismissal. He caught the deferential bow of Amedda's head in the corner of his eye and heard the door hiss as his aide saw himself out.

Whatever it was Skywalker was up to on Naboo, he would

be back soon. He would be hungry for vengeance against Darth Tyranus and eager to restore order to the Republic. The Jedi hadn't completely ruined him for passionate feelings and headstrong action yet, and Palpatine knew exactly what path he wanted to send the boy down next. He called up the specs of the new droid the Separatists were rumored to possess and smiled. The truth was so much better than the rumor. Everything was proceeding as he hoped, and soon enough, he would be able to take his next steps.

⁊⩗⩗⥾

Sabé closed the file on this week's water requisitions for the outlying farms and shut her eyes. It was easy to get lost in the data crunching here, the simple moving around of resources from people who had them to people who needed them. She couldn't pretend that it was galaxy-altering, but it was necessary work, especially for a place like Tatooine that tracked every drop of water. And it soothed her. They were problems she could solve, people she could help. It was easy to get lost in that, to go home at the end of her shift and pretend that was all she was.

She'd never felt like this before, so settled and content doing so little. She'd spent her youngest years pushing herself forward and her teenage years intentionally putting herself to the side. She'd mastered being second best, being the person no one ever saw or remembered. It still surprised her when her neighbors called out to her as she walked home from work in the evening. She could get used to being her own person, doing her own work. She liked it far more than she had expected to.

Yet the mission would always come first. Padmé would always come first. They had promised each other that more than a decade ago, and Sabé was not one to go back on her word without a very good reason. She would continue the work of Padmé's heart here on Tatooine because Padmé couldn't, and if she enjoyed it, so much the better. But she'd always be ready to go if Padmé needed her. Tonra understood that, and so did her boss, even if her boss didn't know exactly who her "offworld contact" was.

They were making good progress on Tatooine. They were becoming trusted members of the community. Even if Sabé had to leave, Tonra could stay and run things on his own for a while. She would be ready for anything, as always.

Sabé opened her eyes. It was time to meet Tonra at the cantina. Her day job was over, and now her other work could begin.

CHAPTER 9

Padmé's communications console chimed, and this time she made herself answer it.

"I don't know why you can't ignore it for just a few more hours," Anakin said when she came back. He was sitting on a divan, looking out over the lake. They hadn't been talking or anything. Just enjoying the quiet.

"I've been ignoring them for days," his wife told him. "At the very least, I have to check and see if it's an emergency."

The past few days had been glorious. They'd gone swimming off one of the rocky promontories near the lake house—avoiding the beach—and spent hours in the sun and water with nothing to worry about except each other and reapplying their sunscreen. They'd climbed one of the mountains behind the house, and Padmé had pointed out the landmarks visible from that great height. They'd lain out on the lanai in the dark, watching the stars, and Anakin had told her about the places he had been while she'd been spending all her time working in the Senate. He hadn't visited all the stars yet, but he was racking up an impressive total.

"I suppose," Anakin said. "Master Obi-Wan is probably wondering what's taking me so long."

"You didn't tell him where you were going?" Padmé asked.

"I said I was escorting you back to Naboo and then I was going somewhere to meditate for a bit," Anakin said. "That's more or less true. He won't worry about me, and I'd know if something was wrong."

"Still, we can't stay here forever," Padmé said.

Anakin wanted to tease her and ask her why not, but he didn't. He knew this was a holiday, and that it had to be over soon.

"I know," he said. "But it was nice while it lasted."

He sat up, bringing in his focus and slowly carving away all the things that distracted him from reality.

"What does Senator Organa want?" he asked.

"How do you know it's him?" Padmé asked. "I get messages from all kinds of people."

"Yes, but the ones from Senator Organa always make you extra thoughtful," Anakin said. "You squinch your nose up, and there's a little line between your eyebrows."

"I do not *squinch*," she said, but she was laughing.

There were really only two politicians Anakin liked. Padmé, because she was beautiful and kind and loved him, and the Chancellor, because he made so much sense. Anakin mostly tolerated the others, but of everyone in Padmé's faction, Bail Organa was his favorite. The man was straight-forward and not given to prevarication to get what he wanted.

"There's a mission," Padmé admitted. "It's quite sensitive, from what I gather, and there can't be any Jedi involved. I don't know the details. Bail can't share them over an insecure link. But I think it's going to be important, and I should get back to Coruscant to help them deal with it."

"All right then," Anakin said. "Here is what I think we should do. We can have one last meal in private together tonight, and then in the morning, you can go back to Theed and take a government ship to Coruscant. I'll make my way back separately."

"Why separately?" Padmé said. "We can travel together. No one will notice."

"I'll notice," Anakin said. "I want our work and our lives to be as separate as possible. Does that make sense? I know you're going to read the whole trip through hyperspace, for example. That doesn't count as time you spend with me."

"I like that," Padmé said. She walked back to the divan and curled up next to him. "Did you read it somewhere?"

"Yes." Anakin blushed. "I had some gaps in my education to fill in."

"I love you," Padmé said.

"I love you, too," he told her.

They sat like that, close together for all the times they

wouldn't be and completely absorbed in each other's company, until C-3PO came out to tell them it was time for dinner.

ᘔᗐᗐᗡ

The journey back to Coruscant was like waking up from a dream. Even Theed, which usually seemed welcoming and small to her these days, had been a bustling mess of noise and people, when all she wanted was the peace of what she'd had by the lake. Her definition of home had shifted, she realized. It was no longer a place, no longer a location she could go to. It was a person. And home would be elusive as long as he was apart from her.

It wasn't all bad. Typho and Dormé were waiting for her at the spaceport. Her new handmaidens, Ellé and Moteé, were there, too. They used the trip to catch everyone up on current policy, which is to say: Padmé and Dormé tried to read as much as humanly possible, and Ellé and Moteé were thrown into the deep end, figuring out where they fitted into the system. C-3PO had come with Padmé, and she'd left R2-D2 with Anakin. She would miss the little astromech, but they had all agreed it would be better for Anakin to have a droid he trusted when the Jedi went to war, and it was safer for C-3PO to join her service.

"I can't believe how quickly the fighting has spread," Padmé said, taking a break from the countless files Bail had sent her. "We've been in conflict with the Trade Federation for a while now, in some form or another, and it always felt so small, like it was just Naboo's problem or just mine. This is so huge."

"I get the impression the Separatists were waiting to make a big move," Dormé said. "Geonosis should have been a victory for them, so their forces were already in place to finish the job."

"Except we got a clone army for the Republic," Padmé mused. "And no one really knows where it came from."

"I heard on a news holo that a Jedi had ordered it years ago," Ellé said. "Admittedly, the holo is somewhat less than reputable, and no one seems to know why a Jedi would do that, but it's the only reasonable theory that's come forward so far."

"The Chancellor seems pleased enough," Moteé added. "He gave command of the army to the Jedi, because the Republic couldn't provide enough generals, but it looks like a move to keep the Senate out of the direct line of power, and the Separatists might . . . appreciate that if it comes to negotiation."

"Do the Jedi even know what to do with an army?" Dormé asked.

"They will soon," Padmé said. "I'm more worried about keeping the Republic together while the war is waged. When things are hard, the Separatists show up with easy solutions. I don't want planets to fall prey to them."

"At least we know what we stand for," said Typho over his shoulder, in the pilot's chair. "That's a start."

It was, at that, and it was better than nothing.

Senator Amidala had the ship land directly at the Senate's port, rather than at her residence. She had been away for long enough that she wanted to get right to work. Ellé and Moteé helped her dress, directed by Dormé, in a more elaborate gown than she usually favored when she went to the Senate. It was time to remind everyone who she was, where she came from, and that she meant business.

Her hair was twisted into two buns just below her ears, and a third at the base of her neck. A thin metal cap lay over her head, decorated with scrolling flowers and vines. Her face was painted pale, not the traditional stark white of Naboo's queen but definitely leaning in that direction. Her lips were stained red and her eyes were shadowed with burgundy powder.

The dress was made of three parts. A Karlini silk underdress that reached below her knees and covered her to the wrists was topped by a heavier tunic-style gown of burgundy velvet. It was sleeveless and extended from her shoulders to the floor in a single, unbroken line that was supported by light steel reinforcements sewn into the fabric. Finally, an elaborately folded white sash nearly half a meter wide was fitted around her waist and extended behind her like a train.

Ellé and Moteé were given purple hooded cloaks to wear over matching dresses. Dormé's head was bare, but she wore the same colors. Typho wore his uniform, his hat tucked smartly under his arm. C-3PO, polished to a gleam, walked with them into the halls of the Senate and remarked that he had, in fact, been made for this.

Dormé and Typho split off, heading for Padmé's office to begin working on her schedule. They took the droid with them. Ellé and Moteé followed Padmé through the corridors as she walked determinedly to her destination. A few people hailed her, but she stopped for none of them. Before long, they arrived at Senator Organa's office.

"Ah, Senator Amidala," Bail said. "It's wonderful to see you. You have recovered from your wounds on Geonosis, then?"

Padmé appreciated his help in disseminating her cover story, even if he hadn't known that was what he was doing. All told, it was pretty close to the truth, except for one glaring omission.

"Yes, thank you, Senator," Padmé said. "The wounds were not deep, but they were in a very awkward place."

"We're glad to have you back," Mon Mothma said. She rose elegantly from her chair to come and shake Padmé's hand. As usual with handmaidens, no one made any mention of Ellé and Moteé, who remained standing by the door.

"I understand there is a mission of some sensitivity to consider?" Padmé said, eager to begin.

"It's endlessly complicated," said Mon Mothma. She linked her arm with Padmé's and led her over to a seat.

Only Bail and Mon Mothma were present, which surprised Padmé. They knew she was coming, and she had expected more of their faction to be in attendance.

"The mission itself is pretty straightforward," Mon Mothma continued. "We have to get a senator and one or two guards onto a specific ship, and then they wait for contact. The issue is that it has to be a senator. Anyone from our faction could go, but we are all busy. Furthermore, the sensitive nature of the venture requires the senator to be unremarkable, and anyone we might send would definitely be missed. We're all too prominent, here. And none of us can be in two places at once."

Bail Organa was too experienced a politician to react if he didn't want to. He wouldn't ask her directly, and he wouldn't give away her secrets. She had always trusted him, but now she knew for sure that her trust had been well placed. He met her gaze evenly, revealing none of her secrets. He was giving her the choice.

"Senators," she said folding her hands together, "if you're looking for someone who can do that, I have the perfect solution for you."

Once there was a girl who worked hard all her life, and this was the part she hated most.

It had been sheer luck that led her to Shmi Skywalker's door. Her portable nav, useful for avoiding the dangers of Tatooine's deserts, had malfunctioned while she was on a supply run in town, and the merchant she'd been bartering with had recommended a place to get it fixed for cheap. Shmi had done the work and been paid, and the girl had returned home unable to get the picture of Shmi's table, covered with parts for tinkering with, out of her mind.

Their network had been interested. Cliegg Lars—after his first conversation with Shmi—even more so.

In the following weeks, Shmi told them all of the Toydarian's weaknesses and the ways he cheated to get around them. She spent most of her time with Cliegg, under the guise of being hired out to tune his moisture vaporators, and he always made her laugh. The rest of the time, she and the girl worked on tracking devices, designed to find a very particular chip.

"Finding it is only half the problem," the girl said. "If we can't deactivate it, what's the point?"

"Everything is solved one step at a time," said Shmi. She was used to small victories.

Finally, the day came: Cliegg lured Watto into a game and beat him, and

Shmi was the promised price. She was free by the time they made it back to the Lars homestead, but her chip stayed where it was.

It took almost three months of trial and error. Shmi would have died had her chip been under the control of an enslaver and not someone who cared about her. It was terrifying to watch, to think about, and yet every day she got up and tried again. The girl did what she could to help, but Shmi's engineering abilities were the best available in their circle.

"I hope you get to meet my son someday," Shmi had said. "I taught him everything I knew, but he was so gifted. He wanted a device like this. It's nice to finish his dream."

At last, the deprogrammer was ready. And all they had to do was test it.

Cliegg couldn't watch. Owen had taken him to the other side of the homestead and tried to keep him distracted. The girl set the device on Shmi's arm and followed the scanner until it located the chip: fused to her lower spine. Once the chip was located, their time was precious. It had to be deactivated before the monitoring device in Cliegg's office realized it was being tampered with. Shmi wouldn't be killed if they failed, but the next person they tried this on wouldn't have the advantage of being free.

The cuts were quick and clean, and soon the girl held the chip in her hand. She bandaged Shmi's back and made sure the blood loss was not significant. They had done it. It had worked.

It didn't work every time.

There was a moment just before a chip's failsafe activated when everyone knew that it had gone wrong. Some screamed. Some closed their eyes and waited. It was always terrible. Shmi worked endlessly to improve the scanner, improve the programming, but she couldn't seem to keep ahead of it.

And then she died.

Cliegg was bereft. Owen was furious, though his fury paled in comparison with that of Shmi's son, who arrived too late to help and left again almost immediately. The girl did the only thing she could: she got up every day and tried again. Others took over the technical aspects of freeing enslaved people on Tatooine, but it was the girl who fed them when they were no longer bound. It was the girl who comforted them if tragedy struck. Most of the newly freed beings left Tatooine, and the girl could not blame them. It wasn't her hands that liberated them, and they might never know her name, but it was her kindness that sent them on their way.

Beru Whitesun knew her work would never be done, but she hoped that it would be enough.

CHAPTER 10

The thing about the water export business was that it was seasonal, and if the season had been poor, there was no water to export. Usually, this resulted in an unwanted loss of a job, but since Sabé wasn't really on Tatooine to ship its already limited resources offworld for profit, being unemployed suited her just fine. Her boss, a decent sort who seemed genuinely sorry she'd brought her all the way out here for nothing, was able to give her a day's work a week monitoring this year's projections. This meant that Sabé, and her ship, had some free time.

The first contact to reach out to them came through Tonra's job at the cantina. Someone needed a few skids of produce sent out to one of the more distant farm holds and was looking for transportation that Tuskens couldn't reach. Sabé made the delivery easily and arranged to make it a monthly occurrence, and after that, jobs began to trickle in.

It wouldn't have been enough to support her if she'd been alone. Tonra's wage at the cantina and her meager salary from the water depot paid the bulk of their bills. But the credits were never the point. Being known as reliable was more important.

Her first offworld job was transporting a family out of the sector. Rather than wait for a public shuttle, they elected to pay her to take them to the closest transportation hub, from which they could charter travel wherever they needed to go. The family were very quiet, very underfed, and carried almost no belongings with them. Sabé did not ask questions, but she didn't really have to. She had hoped that her onworld jobs had been auditions for this one. In the end, she delivered the family safely to the hub, pressed a few extra coins into the hands of the startled adults, and headed back to Tatooine.

Tonra did the next offworld run and reported a similar series of events. His cargo had been three sisters and their children, all of them scrawny and sunburnt. This time, Sabé had packed a kit of food rations and medical supplies for the evacuees to take. She didn't know if the people they ferried would be in touch with their Tatooine contacts again, but she was only half doing it to build up her reputation.

And that was all it took. Two weeks of carefully arranged trips, and Sabon and Arton were known safe harbors in Mos Eisley. It was frustrating, to move so slowly and not see the whole picture, but Sabé told herself that she was doing a better job helping an active system this time. She still had no idea who they were working with, but she knew they were needed and doing a good job.

Tonra had dinner waiting for her when she arrived home from their third offworld run. The food at the cantina where he worked was actually decent, though he tended to add his own seasonings when he brought home takeout.

"That smells amazing," Sabé said, shrugging out of her jacket. "Do I want to know what it is?"

"You do not," Tonra told her. "Just concentrate on how good it smells."

There were a lot of strange reptilian-ish animals on Tatooine, and Sabé had no desire to know which of them she'd eaten.

"I can do that," she said, and took her seat. "Another quiet run today. These ones seemed less timid? Maybe word's getting around that we're safe. One of them almost talked to me."

"They always talk to me," Tonra said, putting a bowl down in front of her. She resisted the urge to stick her tongue out at him. "You have a message from Coruscant."

Only one person would call her from Coruscant, and it wasn't likely that Padmé just wanted to chat. Part of her was thrilled. The work she did on Tatooine was good, but it was a little boring. She missed the high stakes of politics and the thrill of working at a galactic level. A larger part of her was disappointed, which surprised her. She was building something here, and this time they were on the right track. She didn't want to leave *again*.

"I'll eat first," Sabé told him. "Did anything exciting happen while I was away?"

"There was a fight at the cantina this afternoon," Tonra

told her. "Two long-haul traders from the same ship. No one was injured too badly. I think they just wanted to blow off some steam."

He went on to describe the fight in comedic detail, trying to duplicate the voices of the participants, and of his boss, who had tried to keep them from making a mess. Sabé laughed as he spun the yarn, and ate her dinner with a lack of reservation as to what it was.

"If she needs me, you could stay here," Sabé said when he was done telling his story, and trying to eat before his food got cold. He didn't reply immediately. "I mean, if you wanted to. If you'd rather be somewhere else, I understand. But I— Sabon, that is—could just . . . be gone on a longer supply run. And you could keep going with what we're doing here, and then when I'm done, I could come back."

"The thought had occurred," Tonra said. He put his spoon on the table. "I could drop you at the transport hub and keep the ship. We could come up with a story. That way, I could keep doing the runs and just come and get you when you're ready."

"I like that idea," Sabé said. Now that she knew he was on the same page, she was even less ready to pull up stakes in Mos Eisley. "Let me see what she wants before we make any decisions, though."

Sabé took her empty plate and Tonra's and went into the kitchen to wash them. Before, a call from Padmé would have sent her running for the holoprojector, eager to hear what her friend wanted her to do. But something had changed. After Geonosis, Padmé had been uncharacteristically reticent, hiding everything even from Sabé. She'd disappeared to the lake house on Naboo and hadn't contacted anyone for weeks. And yes, Sabé herself wasn't always easy to track down, but Padmé was a senator. If it was important, she found a way. And now she needed Sabé again, and Sabé was alarmed to find she was a little bit resentful. What was happening to them?

When everything was clean, she went to the holoprojector and turned it on. She had no idea what time it was on Coruscant, and she wasn't sure how long she'd have to wait for Padmé to pick up, but someone would be on the other end of the line, and they'd tell her what to expect.

"Sabé!" To her surprise, Padmé's face appeared in front of her almost immediately. The senator looked good, clearly having recovered from whatever happened to her in the droid foundry, and her tone was normal. "Oh, I'm so glad to see you. I've missed you so much."

"I've missed you, too," Sabé said. And it was true. Missing Padmé was like missing the sun, and she was currently on a planet with two of them.

"How is Tatooine?" Padmé asked.

"Hot, dry, and dusty," Sabé told her. "But we're making real progress. The locals, the ones I care about, are starting to trust us. We've already made a few offworld runs for them."

"That's good." Padmé bit her lip. She was definitely going to ask Sabé to leave the planet.

"Tonra suggested that it fits our cover if I disappear on a longer mission," Sabé said. Padmé's relief was immediate. "He'll keep the ship, but I can make it to Coruscant from the transport hub here. When we're done, I can return."

"I'll send Captain Mariek for you," Padmé offered, happy to make everything as easy as she could. "That will make your traveling a bit easier, and I won't worry about you the whole time."

"What do you need me to do?" Sabé asked. She leaned back in her chair, almost relaxed at how familiar this was.

"This one's complicated," Padmé said. "There's a mission my faction in the Senate is running, and it has to be me who goes. Only, I can't disappear from the Senate, because people will notice. I need you to come to Coruscant and be Senator Amidala."

All thoughts of relaxation fled. *Senator* Amidala was so different. There was no makeup to hide behind, no bulky dresses to use as a physical barrier. This wouldn't be a normal switch. She'd have to mimic Padmé on the floor of the Galactic Senate.

"Who knows?" Sabé asked.

"Senator Organa," Padmé said. It wasn't a surprise. He had seen through their disguise early on but had never told anyone about it. Sabé rather liked him. "And Mon Mothma."

That was a very short list, and the Chancellor wasn't on it.

"This is going to be challenging," Sabé said.

"On the bright side, I've just brought on two new hand-maidens," Padmé said. Her voice shuddered a bit referring to the tragedy as a bright side. "You can switch out with one of them easily enough to relearn your way around the Senate, and then you and I can switch places for a couple of days before I leave."

Sabé was already mentally packing her trunk.

"I'll meet Mariek on the transport hub tomorrow, if she can make it," she said.

"I'll make the arrangements," Padmé told her. She hesitated, then smiled. "I am so glad we'll get to see each other again for a bit."

"So am I," said Sabé. It was the truth. "It'll be just like old times. I'd better go pack."

ᔭ ᔎ ᔎ ᔮ

Padmé had been fully intending to tell Sabé the whole story, everything from seeing Anakin again through the time at the Lars homestead and their captivity on Geonosis, including the wedding. But then Sabé had said "just like old times," and her resolve had crumbled.

Anakin hadn't been able to see her when he'd returned to Coruscant. He'd only been on the planet long enough to see the Chancellor, and to get his next assignment before he and Obi-Wan shipped out to the front. They hadn't yet set up a way to communicate surreptitiously, and Padmé had no reason to contact him through official channels. She knew that sort of thing was to be expected; it was why they had traveled separately back from the lake house, but it still stung. She accepted that he would have a job to do, just as she would, but she hadn't expected reality to throw it all in her face quite so quickly. When she had a moment, she would ask C-3PO if there was a way he could securely link to R2-D2.

This time with Sabé was exactly what she needed. She would use it to find her way forward, balancing the old with the new. It *would* be like old times. They would learn to be each other's mirror again, something they hadn't done in years and had never tried on this scale. They would spend time together and it would be easy and fun, and they would have their work to keep them busy. When they had to separate for Padmé to go on the mission, she would know that Sabé would be waiting for her when she came back.

When Sabé arrived, Padmé greeted her with a smile. She introduced her to Ellé and Moteé, and they all sat down with Dormé, Typho, Mariek, and the other guards for the Naboo-style dinner Padmé had planned to welcome Sabé back. There were brightly colored stuffed peppers and five-blossom bread, and berries from the Lake Country soaked in rum custard.

As she watched her friends eat, laughing and talking with one another, Padmé was happy.

She wished Anakin were here. That was the only thing that kept the night from being perfect. She missed him, and not even Sabé could make her feel better. It was strange, to love two people so much, so differently. She didn't quite understand it, and she wasn't sure how to make it work.

Someday, she would figure out how to put both halves of her life together. Someday, she would make the political and the personal more cohesive. Someday, she wouldn't keep them so divided. Someday, Anakin would sit at this table, too. There was a war on, and they were always in danger from that, but there was no reason not to plan for an optimistic future, where every person she had brought into her life was just as happy as everyone else.

CHAPTER 11

The flight to Karlinus was always just long enough to be soothing. It was too short to get any real work done, so Saché always used the time to listen to music and think. Any shorter, and she'd have trouble getting into her head. Any longer, and she'd insist on using the time productively. No, the trip was perfect, and she always arrived feeling refreshed, even when she took the public shuttle, as she did now.

Beside her, her new aide, Tepoh, flipped through a Karlini guidebook. Zhe had left Naboo before but had never visited Karlinus. It was a steep learning curve for this type of diplomatic mission, but Saché knew that anyone who came recommended by Dormé was up to it. When they met, Tepoh had been wearing a flowing green skirt, but today zhe was dressed in dark blue trousers and a silver blazer with matching embroidery.

"What made you want to be a handmaiden?" Saché had asked zher at their interview.

"I didn't, necessarily," zhe replied. "I mean, I didn't know it was a possibility. But when I was recommended for the position, I will admit that I was curious enough to take the interview."

"Someone from the senator's office keeps an eye on everyone in the diplomatic corps," Saché said. "If the proper skill set shows up, she gets a notification."

"I didn't mean my skill set, my lady," Tepoh said. "At the time, I thought they were only looking for girls."

That had given Saché pause. They *had* been looking for girls when Saché was hired. But if someone was willing to play the part sometimes, it didn't really matter what gender they identified as. It would be a job, a disguise. Who she was out of the hood had changed over the years, but she'd always been Saché, even when she served the Queen.

"When the Queen was younger, it was important that her handmaidens be similar to her in appearance," Saché said. "That has changed over the years. Physical resemblance to her is no longer the primary qualification. I think you would have made an excellent handmaiden, and I'm glad you chose to join me."

"I was pleased, too," zhe said. "Sometimes I wake up and I want to be perceived as some degree of female, but sometimes I don't."

"Well," Saché said. "We dressed like that back then to disappear in plain sight. Perhaps Senator Amidala would have wanted you to disappear in other ways that made more sense to your character. She never asked me to do anything that was against mine, for example, even when we were young and still figuring each other out."

Tepoh paused to consider that and smiled.

"I think I would have enjoyed it," zhe said. "Maybe they would have let me wear a guard uniform sometimes. Those are quite dashing. But I think I'll be happier with you. It took me some time to figure myself out, and I think I'll serve Naboo better this way. I like being myself."

"I was only twelve when Captain Panaka recruited me," Saché said. Sometimes, those ten years felt like a lifetime. She'd changed so much since then. "At the time, being part of the Queen's retinue was all I wanted. I was sorry to leave her, when her terms were finished, even though I had just won my own election. But now I think you're correct. There's a lot to be said for being yourself. Not everyone is meant to be a shadow."

Tepoh smiled.

In front of them, Karlinus grew larger and larger. Its waters were a different shade of blue than Naboo's, but it was as green and growing. The planet was a little bit warmer and much more humid, meaning large parts of it could be used for growing the tea and raising the silkworms Karlinus was renowned for. There was still plenty of room for the grain fields, too. Karlinus was, of all the Chommell sector planets, the closest to being self-sufficient. Even Naboo relied on an influx of workers, while Karlinus could support itself if it had to.

Saché had not expected Governor Kelma to meet them at the public space platform, and indeed she did not, but Saché was pleasantly surprised to see the person who *was* there to greet them.

"Harli Jafan!" she said, extending a hand for the other young woman to shake. "I haven't seen you in forever."

"It's Saché, correct?" Harli said. "Forgive me, but I always mix the lot of you up."

"That is entirely understandable," Saché said. "We went to a great deal of trouble to make that happen."

"I'm pretty sure I tried to kiss the wrong one of you once," Harli said. "And because I was a teenager, I reacted poorly to the rejection."

Saché remembered that incident quite clearly and winced.

"It's all water under the bridge now," Harli assured her. "Who is this?"

"This is Tepoh, my new aide," Saché said. "Zhe has never been to Karlinus before, but I have high hopes for zher."

"A pleasure," said Harli, shaking Tepoh's hand. "Whatever she tells you about me being a bad influence, it is not true."

"Oh, so it was someone else who arranged for us to sneak out of Theed palace to see that concert?" Saché said. "I had the most mortifying evening of my life as a result of that caper. I'm pretty sure I remember who had the idea."

"Hey, I just said I had tickets." Harli laughed. Tepoh was looking at both of them with something like shock on zher face. "You are the ones who managed to get out of the palace."

"That much is true," Saché said. It had been ages since she'd thought about that night. In hindsight, it was quite funny. The expression on Panaka's face when he'd realized what the blood was the result of!

"I think we're scandalizing your aide," Harli said. "We all know that Queen Amidala would *never*."

Saché laughed, which did not reassure Tepoh at all, and picked up her traveling case.

Harli led the way to her transport, and they made their way to the governor's house, where they would be staying. Harli was quartered there, too, of course. Technically, she outranked Saché by quite a bit, being the heir to her planet's ruling family, but the Jafans never acted very formally, unless they needed something.

The streets in Karlini City were wide avenues, with plenty of space for vehicles and pedestrian traffic. The buildings were sided with metal slats, which reflected the sun's heat and kept the interiors a bit cooler. The whole effect was rather dazzling, as the light gleamed off the buildings. Saché found she couldn't look at anything too directly and wondered if she had packed goggles or something. She swore it hadn't been this bright the last time she was here. At least the road in front of them was easy to look at.

Tepoh was looking at everything. Zhe didn't seem to mind the glare at all, and was peering curiously at the buildings, shops, and street-level infrastructure with equal levels of interest. Saché was generally happy with her life, but in that moment she missed traveling to new worlds and seeing new places.

The governor's house was not metal-plated but instead built in an older style. Its architecture was quite similar to Naboo's at first glance, all sweeping curves and gentle domes. A closer view, however, immediately made the differences apparent. The native rock on Karlinus was less dense than the granite used to build on Naboo, so they could make their buildings different shapes without the same external support buttresses. There was a delicacy to Karlini architecture that Naboo could only achieve by cheating and using technology.

And then, of course, there was the silk. Every window was hung with it, curtains of every color imaginable, and there were flags lining the roof. The combination of soft wind-blown silk and hard steady rock gave the whole house a rather ethereal feel, as though real and not real things overlapped to keep it standing. The effect was marvelous.

Governor Kelma was waiting for them at the top of the steps. She was a decade older, too, but her golden-brown skin was still unlined, and her long hair was still as dark and thick as ever. She smiled as they approached.

"Representative Saché, how wonderful to see you again," the governor declared. "Welcome to Karlinus, and to my house. And welcome, too, young person. How may I address you?"

"My name is Tepoh," the aide said, clearly surprised to be spoken to directly. It was, after all, zher first day at work. "I'm the representative's new aide."

"Tepoh is a new addition to my staff," Saché explained, "but honestly, I don't know how I got by without zher. The travel here, alone, was much more organized than usual, and my things were all packed before I knew I was leaving."

That was a slight exaggeration, but Tepoh still preened to hear it.

"Please, please, come in," Kelma said. "I'm going to have my people take your things up to your rooms, but if you don't mind, I'd like to get right to work. I've had some lunch brought in."

"That's perfectly fine," Saché said. "I want to get to the bottom of this as quickly as possible, too. Tepoh, could you get my—"

She turned and found her aide already holding the official legislative recording device she was about to request, along with her personal datapad and stylus.

"See," she told zher, "I told you."

They followed the governor through the wide hallways of the public part of her house. Saché knew there was a ballroom and an extensive library—housing mostly public documents— as well as a recreational center and a theater. There were also several meeting rooms, and it was to the largest of these that they were shown. The room was not full, fortunately. It seemed that the governor was going to keep these talks relatively small. But this was the most secure place in the public house. A table was set up with ten place settings. Harli had a staff with her, of course, and Kelma had several aides, as well. Saché did not feel outnumbered.

As they ate, Governor Kelma outlined her planet's main concerns with the old bill. None of it was a particular surprise, but Saché was more than happy to hear her perspective.

"We did some digging," Kelma said. "It turns out the bill has been contested since the day it was signed. Karlini settlers, and those from other planets, felt the terms were unfair. In particular, the part where it never expired."

"Jafan is, as you can imagine, also not happy with it," Harli said. "Something like that could bankrupt us overnight."

"I'm here to make sure it's never invoked," Saché said. "I don't mind telling you that I think it's abhorrent, and I would never vote to support it. Naboo is not self-sufficient, but there's no good reason to exploit another planet to cover our own weak spots in a crisis. My goal is to strike the bill entirely."

"Yet you had to come here," the governor said. "Rather than just tell us it was done."

Saché ground her teeth.

"There is a faction, a small one, that is allowing their fear to rule them," she admitted. "They don't want the bill to disappear entirely. They remember the suffering during the

Occupation, and they want to be able to avoid it, during the escalating Clone War."

"Jafan will not allow itself to be exploited," Harli declared. "And it will defend other planets, too."

"I don't doubt it," Saché said. "What I am here to do is work out a plan with you that I can take back to my government and present as a compromise. I don't think they really care what I end up with. They just want to have something to replace the bill we're scrapping."

"I don't like this very much," Kelma said.

"I don't, either," Saché said. "But I am choosing to look at it as an opportunity. Naboo has, from time to time, taken advantage of every planet in the Chommell sector. We can end that, if we set our minds to it. We can come up with something so mutually beneficial, the Naboo government will beg to sign it, and then you'll be safe from us while still enjoying the things we can produce."

"I've missed your aggressive optimism," Harli said. "Sabé was like that, too."

"It was a job requirement," Saché said. She held out her hand, and Tepoh passed her the stylus and datapad. "Shall we get to work?"

CHAPTER 12

Coruscant had not improved since the last time Sabé was there. No sooner had they landed than she felt the oppressive weight of all the people, the strange dichotomy of so much life without anything natural. Everything on Coruscant was a construct, built on layers of what had come before: erasing, covering, destroying, all in the name of reaching ever farther up. She could tell Padmé was happy, so she put her best face on and found she genuinely enjoyed the welcome dinner. It was good to see everyone again, good to be part of a big team again, even if a few of the faces were unfamiliar.

Ellé and Moteé were, of course, brilliant girls with a wide independent streak. They were not afraid to show initiative, but they didn't thrive on the recognition of it. That was something Sabé was intimately familiar with. Ellé was a former aide to Governor Bibble, good-naturedly poached from his service. Moteé was a recent graduate of the political academy in Theed. Dormé had done excellent work recruiting them. Sabé noticed that both of the new aides were more politically inclined than the previous handmaidens had been. She said as much to Dormé quietly between courses as Padmé's new protocol droid cleared the dishes.

"Yes," Dormé said. "We decided that a focus on Senate service was needed. I have a small staff of my own, now, to deal with the more domestic side of the senator's life here. They dress and look like handmaidens, but Padmé decided to separate her household a little bit, going forward."

It made sense. Their old scheme, the decoy queen, had been entirely built around misdirection. Padmé had changed it when she became senator, and changing it again as her needs shifted was logical. It did make Sabé's job more difficult, though. Sabé needed to learn a new system that wasn't designed for a body double, and then she'd have to be a body double without any of the full-face makeup tricks they used to use. Her sun- and wind-scoured skin was the least of her problems. As she and Padmé had grown older, they'd grown more physically distinct. Fortunately, Dormé was incredibly skilled with contouring.

The new system would also, Sabé realized, allow Padmé to separate her work life from her time at home. Before, she had lived and breathed politics all the time, with her handmaidens always at the ready to support her. Now, with Dormé as the only crossover point, she could leave work at the Senate building, as much as she wanted. It was a freedom Padmé had never sought before, and Sabé could only wonder what had changed.

Because she *had* changed. That much was sure. Padmé's

smile was a little too bright, her eyes too engaged in the conversations around the table. Sabé knew Padmé's face as well
as she knew her own, and she could tell that, for whatever
reason, Padmé was playing a role tonight. It wasn't usually
something she did amongst friends. Maybe it had something to
do with the mission Bail was sending her on. In any case, Sabé
wouldn't ask. Padmé would tell her, if she needed to know,
and they'd incorporate it into the disguise, same as before.

Padmé caught her eye across the dessert course, mask
dropping for a moment as she smiled. It was good to be home.

It took three days for Padmé to carve out enough time to brief
Sabé properly. She wanted to do it in private, and since the
whole process was clandestine, she couldn't drop out of any of
her previous engagements. There were long days at the Senate
and long nights in committee meetings or, worse, at parties
garnering support. With Dormé to ensure she looked the part,
and Ellé and Moteé to record, observe, and memorize, Padmé
was able to plan her mission even as she pretended everything
was normal. Still, her distraction meant that the bulk of the
physical work fell to Captain Typho.

"You're disturbingly good at that," Typho said as Sabé
presented him with false identification for both himself and
the senator.

"You learn a few things when you're trying to combat traffickers," Sabé replied. She winked at him. He had no idea.

When she wasn't helping Typho, Sabé was far from idle. She learned how both aspects of Padmé's new life functioned, doubling for both her in-residence handmaidens and accompanying the senator to work. She spent hours with Dormé, learning faces and names and affiliations. She even spoke with Senator Organa twice. Both calls were seemingly innocuous, one to welcome her to Coruscant and one to inquire about how many people Senator Amidala would be bringing to a dinner party.

She thought she might claw her way out of her skin. Somewhere on Tatooine, Tonra was so close to a major operation, and she was here, spinning her wheels over invitations. She knew Padmé's tasks were important, but it was strange to step back into the senatorial role when she'd just gotten used to her place on Tatooine.

At last, on the third day, Padmé arrived home from the Senate with no plans for the evening and decided to go to bed early. She dismissed everyone but Sabé, and the two of them settled in to talk.

"You're much more popular than you were the last time I was here." Sabé had a comb in one hand and was carefully taming the snarls left behind by Padmé's various hairpins, trying to preserve her curls. "I haven't read a single tall tale about you in three days."

"Thank goodness for that," Padmé said. "Though the news is all about the war, these days. I almost wish my supposed scandals were the only things for the 'casters to talk about."

She relaxed in her chair while Sabé's careful hands untangled her hair. Maybe after all of this, she'd switch to plain styles entirely. Or at the very least, give up on the headpieces.

"I like the new guy," Sabé said. "His voice is soothing even though his headlines are all sensationalized. I know that some of it is propaganda, but he feels consistent."

She started to braid Padmé's hair. It wasn't easy to find a practical hairstyle that Padmé could do herself and fitted under a flight helmet, so they were practicing. Multitasking. It really was like old times.

"A coronet would be the easiest, but I can't fit that under the helmet," Padmé grumbled. "Maybe we should cut it?"

"Dormé would kill me," Sabé said. "Give me more than five minutes, and if it gets really bad, we'll send a message to Rabé."

"I would never dream of interrupting an important musician for hair advice." Padmé laughed.

Sabé began work on a second braid.

"I've picked up quite a bit of information about the mission already, I think," she said. "Between what you were able to tell me on the call and what I've gotten from the questions Senator Organa didn't ask me, anyway."

"I still wanted to tell you the full plan myself," Padmé said. "Without interruption, if possible."

"I appreciate it," Sabé said. "Even though we did train in espionage together."

"There are a bunch of new corporations that are shuttling supplies and necessities through the war zone, particularly in the Mid Rim," Padmé said. "A lot of them are just regular merchants who repurposed when the war broke out, but it all happened so fast that no one really knows who works for whom."

"You mean, you suspect some of them are double-dipping?" Sabé asked. "Selling to both sides and making a profit?"

"That's basically unavoidable." Padmé grimaced. "We can't stop it or control it, but we're hoping we can direct contracts toward people we trust."

Sabé tied off the second braid and started on a third.

"What about arms?" she asked. "And smuggling?"

"There's that, too, of course," Padmé said. "Senator Organa thought we would have to conduct an official investigation eventually. We just don't have time right now, because we're trying to marshal everyone else."

Padmé's personal communication device had been flashing nonstop since the senator sat down, and she was resolutely ignoring it. She'd have to go back to work eventually, but when she'd said no interruptions, she'd meant it.

"And then we got, for lack of a better term, an invitation," Padmé said. "The Jedi received a tip about one of the corporations who wanted to meet with a senator in person, but privately. It's too good an opportunity to pass up—to see the inner workings of our supply chain in such a direct manner—but we still have to be discreet about it."

"And that's where we come in," Sabé said. "How do you know the tip is good?"

"We don't," Padmé said. "But it's a good lead, and the ship that Captain Typho found for us is as safe as he can make it. It used to be an independent contractor that did short-haul medical transportation, but now it's been converted to transport medical supplies, and they work freelance for the corporation."

"I am just imagining the ulcer Quarsh Panaka would be getting right now," Sabé said. It was still strange to her that he wasn't around.

"Mariek Panaka is fine with it," Padmé said. If she was upset, it didn't show. "Also, the captain is a Wookiee. I always feel safe around Wookiees for some reason."

Sabé finished a fourth braid and began to roll them into coils that rested on the back of Padmé's neck. The space between the collar of her flight suit and the bottom of her helmet was all they had to work with, so the coils were tight. Padmé touched the tray of beads she usually wore when her hair was done up for flying. It was the easiest style, but it wasn't the easiest to do on the back of her own head. She missed Cordé. The jewelry her handmaiden had left behind was a cold replacement for her presence.

"Where's your helmet?" Sabé asked when she was done.

"In the closet," Padmé said. She waited while Sabé retrieved it, and then tried it on.

"Well, that's as good as we're going to get, I think," Sabé said, making a few quick adjustments to the coils. "Now take that off, and we'll see if you can replicate it."

Padmé meant to tell her. She really did. But it was so comfortable. So familiar. They were planning and working together, and Padmé was reluctant to spoil that with new information, especially something so volatile. There would be time later. There would always be time for the two of them.

⟋⋁⋁⋁⟍

"Don't you ever get tired of that?" Obi-Wan Kenobi asked as his lightsaber blade vanished into the hilt. Around him, the sound of fighting did not cease. There were multiple engagements nearby, and the smell of burning ozone indicated that the air battle proceeded, as well.

"Why would I?" Anakin was surrounded by half-smelted metal, as several dismembered battle droids were crumpled on the ground around him.

This wasn't their first encounter with the Separatist forces on this planet. It wasn't even their first encounter today. And yet every time, Anakin leapt into the thick of the battle, his lightsaber ignited and his movements deadly sharp. Obi-Wan followed, but he didn't have the same enthusiasm his Padawan seemed to feel. Maybe they would balance each other out. Their clone troopers were finishing up their own skirmish a few meters away. Combining tactics was still a work in progress.

"You could at least look less cheerful about it," Obi-Wan said.

"We're doing our jobs, Master," Anakin said. "We're helping people who need it and restoring justice and order. What is not to like?"

Four clones did not get up. That did darken Anakin's face. A fifth trooper went to stand near her fallen comrades. She took her helmet off, long dark braids shaking loose. Anakin watched as she placed each trooper's hands on his chest.

"We can pick them up on our way out," he said.

"Thank you, sir," the trooper said. "We leave our brothers' helmets where they fall."

Anakin watched as she took each helmet and lined them up underneath a nearby tree. It wasn't much of a monument, but it was better than nothing. Clone armor took a very long time to degrade. Anyone who came this way in the next decade or so would know.

"What's your name, trooper?"

"Sister," she said. "It's how my brothers tell everyone I belong."

"Belonging is important," Anakin said. He knew that better than most.

"I was afraid, before I left Kamino," Sister said. "We don't really know what happens to unusual clones. But my brothers never let me doubt. I wasn't sure if the Jedi would understand."

"The Jedi are all about transcending things," Anakin said. "I don't think we can complain if you've transcended gender."

"Transcended gender," Sister said. "We'll work on it, but I like where it's heading."

Anakin laughed. He liked the clones, all of them. They were developing individuality quickly, and it made Anakin feel more comfortable fighting alongside them. He understood droids, and knew better than most how to work with them, but he preferred people now that he was in a position to protect them. Also, they were so much more fun than the Jedi, and their approach to life—to war—was much more similar to his own.

"Let's get back before General Kenobi thinks we've deserted," he said.

Obi-Wan had gone to talk to Commander Cody, R2-D2 trailing behind him. The droid didn't seem to mind the rocky terrain, toddling along slowly but surely.

"I wish we had better cover," Obi-Wan mused, looking out

at the rocky plain and wishing for more than the occasional bantha-sized boulder. "I hate losing troopers like this."

Cody nodded. Clone production continued now that the war was fully engaged. The Republic needed more troops. The Republic also, in Obi-Wan's opinion, needed more generals, but no one had asked him about that. At the very least, he could tell the Jedi Council that Anakin was ready for the trials. They would still stay together as often as possible if Obi-Wan could arrange it, but Anakin would have his own troopers and a higher rank. It wasn't done very often, but these were unusual circumstances, and Obi-Wan was sure that Anakin was up to the task.

Commander Cody sounded an alarm along their secure comm: more Separatist droids were incoming. Obi-Wan watched as Anakin lifted one of the massive boulders. One of Cody's troopers covered him. Anakin threw the rock directly into the approaching ranks as his opening salvo. It was effective, if a little bit showy.

They would talk about it later.

CHAPTER 13

The ship Captain Typho had selected for their mission was a Wookiee vessel called the *Namrelllew*. Padmé and Typho were due to report on board in two more days. Their official job was to ensure the safe delivery of the supplies the *Namrelllew* was carrying: the merchants aboard were seasoned spacers but less accustomed to doing any fighting. Thus, Padmé and Typho would be responsible for the physical safety of the crew and the cargo, while the crew would be in charge of operations. Padmé could easily imagine the expression on Captain Panaka's face at the idea of them being at the mercy of unknown beings to get them safely to their destination. But she was older now, and more experienced, and she knew how to take precautions without his oversight.

Accordingly, Padmé selected her Naboo pilot uniform for travel. It wasn't a particularly recognizable livery and even less so once she had stripped all the heraldry and Naboo-specific design elements off. She spent an evening distressing the leather trousers and tunic, making them appear more worn than they were without compromising their defense design. Typho was quite pleased to leave his uniform hat behind, also choosing the modified Naboo pilot gear. They could wear helmets on the slight chance they came across anyone who would recognize their faces, and they would have a secure comlink between just the two of them. Padmé tried very hard not to think about what had happened the last time she and Typho wore these disguises. At least this time she was putting only him at risk, not anyone else.

She intentionally did not use C-3PO to reach out to Anakin. She considered it at some length, trying to come up with a suitable code and even drafting a few messages, but in the end she decided against it. Yes, he was her husband, but she was a senator, and this was her job. The mission was need-to-know, and strictly speaking, he didn't need to know. The only reason she had to tell him was that they were married, and their marriage was a secret. She would treat him the way she would if they were nothing to each other. It was not an easy call to make, and she was sure it wouldn't be the last time she did it. She knew he would understand. He would have to keep Jedi missions a secret from her, as well, and she understood that perfectly.

It was harder than she thought, balancing a new marriage with her work. She didn't have a lot of time to establish new habits, and therefore it was easier to just keep everything a secret. Once she started explaining things—to Anakin or to Sabé—she felt like she might never stop. She didn't have time for that right now, so she opted to hold everything back. After this mission, surely, things would be quiet for long enough that she could hammer out some details with Anakin about their procedures and tell Sabé all of her good news.

She didn't enjoy keeping secrets from those she loved, of course, but it was the easiest path for now. The war couldn't last for very long. The Republic would help the Separatist planets understand that people like the Trade Federation did not have their best interests at heart, and then the conflict would be over. Too many good people were working on solutions, too many good people wanted peace, for the war to drag on. She was an idealist, and she wasn't about to change that now. The artist Kharl was right: it was time to bring a little bit of Naboo to the rest of the galaxy.

The night before they were due to depart, Senator Amidala attended the opera with Senator Organa. She brought two handmaidens along with her, both hooded in muted tones of green and burgundy. The senator wore a dress of deep green, embroidered with sea-green highlights that wove vines of some imaginary plant around her form. The long skirt was heavy, supported underneath by a blaster-proof petticoat. The bodice was a touch less formal than anything she might have worn on the Senate floor, leaving the tops of her shoulders exposed, even though the stomacher near came up to her collarbones. Her hair was down, but woven through it were the same vines from her dress, making it look like they were all attached at the root.

The senator spoke to everyone with all of her usual grace and passion, letting no one give her easy answers, even though they were gathered together for a night of art appreciation. Anyone who hoped to get a hint of Senate proceedings out of her was left wanting, and anyone she asked for an update on their efforts for the war answered fully. She didn't have a hair or a brushstroke out of place, the perfect living symbol of everything the Republic could be if they all fought to stay together.

Sabé was deeply uncomfortable the entire time, even with Bail along to cover any introductions she might mess up.

Dormé had done a wonderful job with the makeup. Sabé was still a little sand blown from her time on Tatooine, but color and contouring had turned her face into the perfect match for Senator Amidala. They had added extensions to her hair, melding the new lengths seamlessly with the shorter style she favored these days. This was Sabé as she could be, if she wanted, always right next to the very thrum of galactic power.

During the intermission, half a dozen strangers-to-Sabé filled Senator Organa's box to pay their respects. As Amidala, she was gracious and polite, if perhaps a little bit aloof. When the lights began to darken again, Sabé was relieved, and not just because she'd missed the entire last three seasons of Alderaanian opera and was excited to catch up.

"It gets better," Bail whispered in her ear. She wasn't sure at first if he meant the opera or the political maneuvering. Possibly he meant both. She was more out of practice with the niceties of politics than she'd thought she was. Or, more accurately, perhaps she was starting to grow past her tolerance for them. "You're doing an outstanding job."

Sabé reached one hand back to where the handmaidens were seated, and Padmé squeezed her fingers. They would be apart soon, driven by the mission and their duties and loyalties. She trusted Bail. She trusted Padmé's vision. She was even starting to trust Coruscant, as much as it galled her. It was good to be working with her friends again.

First the steamer blew a gasket, and then the coolant leaked out of the refrigeration units, and *then* six rowdy podrace hotheads showed up fifteen minutes before the cantina was supposed to close. The comedy of errors did not help Captain Tonra pose as Arton Dakellan, but it didn't make it impossible for him to maintain his cover. Mostly he just did whatever he could to save their food stores while reassuring the cook that it was going to be all right if the hotheads could have only a limited menu. He may have threatened them. Just a little bit.

By the time everything was said and done, Tonra was so behind schedule getting back to the apartment that he only stopped to throw a long tunic over his work uniform. He had planned to change entirely and also to eat something, but now all he could do was grab a bag of their emergency rations and head to the ship.

He finally arrived at the pickup coordinates, almost an hour and a half late. No one was waiting for him, but he landed anyway. Perhaps there would be a message.

Like every one of their meeting spots on Tatooine, it was a sand dune in a sea of dunes. Tonra knew the planet had rocks and cliffs and that sort of thing, but for whatever reason all of their contacts met them in the desert. He'd given up cleaning his boots.

By the time he disembarked, a droid was waiting for him at the bottom of the ramp. There had never been a droid before. It was a simple humanoid model from the waist up and set on triangular treads instead of legs. Clearly home-made, or at least highly modified. Tonra stood still while the droid scanned him, confirming his identity. Then he spoke.

"I'm sorry," he said. "I couldn't get away from town without causing a fuss, and I didn't think that would be . . . desired."

"Your discretion is appreciated," the droid said.

That was something, at least. He was used to the chain of command, but not having enough information to know when a little creative rule breaking would be warranted was driving him around the bend.

"Is it possible for you to tell me why the timeline is so tight?" he asked. "It might help me avoid this happening again, that's all."

"I am unable to do that," the droid said. "Please wait a moment."

Tonra waited. A figured stepped out from behind one of the dunes and walked toward him. They appeared human, or at least humanoid. They were deeply cowled—which was not unusual in the desert—and Tonra didn't even try to get a closer look at their face.

"Arton Dakellan," the figure said through a voice modulator. "You and your wife are relative newcomers to Tatooine."

"We are," Tonra said. He had no idea how long you had to live here before you were considered a local, but he assumed it was longer than the time he and Sabé had spent.

"Did you come here to help us?" they asked.

It was an oddly general question that could have meant almost anything, but Tonra knew what he wanted it to mean, and that was the answer he gave.

"We did," he said. "We knew it was a possibility when we came here, and we hoped to be useful."

The figure considered him for a moment and then seemed to arrive at a decision.

"Each enslaved being on Tatooine has been implanted

with a chip, capable of killing them instantly if they break any rule or attempt to free themselves." Tonra nodded, and the figure continued. "We have a device that allows us to deactivate the chips, but it's tricky. What works on the first chip will no longer work by the tenth."

"My cargo!" Tonra was alarmed. "Are they—"

"They are well enough," the figure told him. "We must reprogram the device on our end, before we make another attempt, any other attempt. Are either you or your wife slicers?"

"We have some skill," Tonra said. "And we have access to very good equipment."

The figure didn't ask what those resources might be. Clandestine work was equal parts thrilling and frustrating, and right now Tonra was somewhere between the two. But again, he knew better than to push. They had pushed the first time they'd been on Tatooine, and it had gotten them closed doors. This time, they had promised each other, they would take it slow and let the locals come to them.

"Take this." The figure passed him a crude-looking scanning device and a bag that clinked dully when Tonra shifted it. "It's one of our chip deactivators and some testing blanks. See if you can make any modifications to improve it."

"We'll do our best," Tonra said. He turned the device over in his hands. It was quite haphazard.

"You should have seen the first one," the figure said. "It was mostly made out of kitchen appliances."

"Needs must," Tonra said quietly.

"Indeed," the figure said. "We will be in touch, Arton Dakellan."

"Thank you for your trust," Tonra said.

The figure nodded and disappeared again behind the dune. Tonra heard no speeder, but there were plenty of other ways to cross the Tatooine sands, especially if one favored stealth over speed.

He walked onto the ship and checked the chronometer. It was late in Theed, but not too late for him to try. He activated the holoprojector and waited, wishing deeply that Versé were still alive for him to call. Several of the handmaidens were slicers, but Versé had been the uncontested best.

"Captain?" the familiar form of music sensation Rabé Tonsort flickered into view in front of him.

"Hello, Rabé," he said fondly. "Do you have a moment?"

"I always have a moment for old friends," she said. "What have you got?"

"You are aware of our current project?" he asked.

"Yes," she said. "And that you are currently operating solo."

"Right," he said. "This device is used to deprogram chips, but the chips have a self-replicating defensive code. Every time it gets used, it only works for so long. We're hoping to make it more flexible and more powerful."

"Is that a pair of pruning shears?" Rabé squinted as she peered at the object he held in his hand.

"Possibly," Tonra said. "They work with what they can get for the mechanical aspects, and that helps them conceal what they're doing. It's the technical side the device is weak on."

"Send me the specs and I'll see what I can do," Rabé said.

"Thank you," Tonra said. "I know you have a lot of things on your plate right now."

"Please," Rabé said. "The day I can't prep for a planetwide concert and slice code at the same time is the day I retire. Say hello to Sabé for me when she gets back. Tell her I love her."

"I'm sure she'd say the same to you," Tonra said, and disconnected the call.

Without the blue light of Rabé's hologram, the cargo bay was suddenly very dark, so Tonra climbed up to the flight deck, where the moonlight streamed through the windows. He examined the device in his hands again. It was brilliant, really. Simple and basically effective. Easy to hide. If he could improve it, even a little bit, it would make a difference. And that was why they'd come back to Tatooine. What they'd hoped for. This was how they would make the galaxy a better place.

The only thing missing was Sabé.

CHAPTER 14

The first day of meetings on Karlinus was not as productive as Saché might have hoped. She wasn't entirely surprised, though. She'd been in politics a long time, and she knew exactly what kind of leader Harli Jafan was. Besides, she was on a fact-finding mission as much as anything else, so it wasn't really a problem to listen patiently while the other Chommell sector leaders aired their grievances. It was just frustrating.

At least Governor Kelma didn't spend the afternoon yelling at her. Harli was passionate and fiery, and only had one volume when it came to public speaking. She was determined that her planet would not be taken advantage of again, and as Saché listened to the details of what Naboo had taken for its own under the existing contract, she could understand the rage. Kelma's approach was a bit more placid, but equally damning. There could be no denying it: the legislation that existed favored Naboo in the extreme, and it would have to be changed as soon as possible, or conflict would tear the sector apart.

They broke for an early dinner once Kelma decided that enough dirty laundry had been aired for the day.

"It will give you an idea of the response your amendments will receive," she said to Saché as she stood up. "Anything short of a complete removal will be met with considerable ire."

"I understand," Saché said. "Thank you for giving me some extra time to think about it."

Beside her, Tepoh was taking notes at near lightspeed on zher datapad. Saché's aide was in trousers again today, but the tunic zhe wore over them was long and flowing, falling almost to zher knees. Tepoh always had a seemingly inexhaustible number of pockets and was able to store and monitor all of zher devices as well as Saché's while they worked, freeing Saché up to engage completely with the other delegates. It was a very efficient system. Saché hoped zhe never planned to quit.

"Representative Saché?" Kelma said, before Saché could decide what to do next. "If you don't mind, I have a secondary reason for calling today's talks a bit short. There is something I would like you to see. As . . . a friend of the Queen's."

"Of course," Saché said. "Tepoh, why don't you go back to our quarters. You've spent far too long looking at screens today. Rest a bit, and then maybe take a tour of the gardens?"

Tepoh was new to politics, but zhe wasn't that naïve. Zhe took no offense at the abrupt dismissal.

"Of course," zhe said, and left the room.

Harli was also alone now, having dismissed her aides. She clearly had no idea what Kelma was talking about and was just as clearly not going to miss out.

"If you'll follow me, then," Kelma said, and led the way through the house to the back exit and her private vehicle hangar.

"There have been two major changes to the Karlini economy since the war began," Kelma said. She unlocked the speeder, and they all got in. Saché put on a pair of goggles, though the other two women chose not to. "Our export of tea has almost doubled, and it's not going to the Core like usual."

"Who's the buyer?" Harli asked, fastening her restraint.

"I'm not entirely sure," Kelma said. "The purchases are made from the farmers directly, which is interesting, because it guarantees the most profit for them."

"Do you mind not getting a cut?" Harli asked.

"They pay their taxes," Kelma said. "And it makes them happy. It all evens out eventually."

She put the speeder in reverse, and they pulled out of the hangar and onto the main road.

"Can your workforce keep up?" Saché asked.

Despite the initiative set in motion when Amidala was queen, the number of Naboo artists who chose to make their start-up credits harvesting tea and silk on Karlinus was dwindling. Without that influx of workers, more and more of production fell to the droid workforce. They were competent, but without organic oversight, the delicacy of both tea and silk would suffer.

"That would be the second change," Kelma said. "We're having an influx of workers, too."

"Where are they from?" Saché asked, and then corrected herself. "I'm sorry, I know your immigration policy doesn't work that way."

Karlinus accepted everyone who arrived to work as a citizen immediately, so they didn't keep records about where people came from.

"It's all right," Kelma said. They passed through the city gates, and into the countryside. Kelma turned east and sped up. "There was some talk about changing the entry process just for the stochastic reasons, but it's taking a while because most of the legislatures feel it's a breach of privacy."

"Has anyone asked?" Harli said drily.

"No," said Kelma. "It is my first day running a planet."

Harli snorted.

"They're family groups for the most part," Kelma said. "Not always the same species, but they tend to arrive in clusters. They're shy. They're afraid of the government. And they are deeply, deeply surprised at how much they get paid."

"They were enslaved," Saché said. "And now they're free."

"That's my operating hypothesis," Kelma said. "I've avoided official visits, but since the two of you are here, I wanted to let you know about it."

"Is Sabé sending them to you?" Saché asked.

Harli's eyes widened.

"No," Kelma said. "Or at least she hasn't said anything. I haven't heard from her since the original twenty-five she brought here, what, six years ago?"

"Something like that," Saché said.

"Why is Sabé involved at all?" Harli asked.

"It began as a special project for Senator Amidala," Saché told her. "She was on Tatooine when Padmé first joined the Senate. She had to leave, but she's spent quite a bit of time there in the intervening years. She said there was a system on Tatooine already, and that ignoring it the first time had gotten her in trouble, so this time she was going to take it slow."

The speeder arrived at a neat little village on the edge of a wide plateau of tea plants. Irrigation droids hovered over the fields. There were no harvest droids out. It was too early in the season. The houses were small but well kept, and most of them had little gardens with bright flowers or painted glass windows so that the light inside would be kaleidoscopic. As they got out of the speeder, a tall Rodian woman approached them.

"Sabé?" she said, surprised. A child tore past her, heading straight for Saché, only to pull up short when she realized her mistake.

"You're not Sabé," the little girl said.

"No," Saché said. "My name is Saché. Sabé is one of my best friends."

"Well, that's good," the child said. She returned to her mother.

"Saché is also married to Yané," Kelma said gently. "One of the people who helped you settle in."

"Oh, I remember her," the Rodian said. "She was delightful."

"I am rather fond of her," Saché said, and smiled.

"My name is Harli, if anyone is interested," Harli said. Then she remembered her manners. "You have a very lovely village."

"Thank you," said the Rodian. "My name is Xeebi, and I have lived here for six years. I assume you are here about the new arrivals?"

"Unofficially, I assure you," Kelma said. "You know better than most that Amidala takes a personal interest in your people here, and even though she is now the Naboo senator, she thinks of you as her responsibility."

"In that case, I am happy to invite you all into my house," Xeebi said. "Though of course what my neighbors wish to tell you will be up to them."

"I understand," Saché said. "Thank you for the welcome."

Saché wished that Tepoh had accompanied her, or at least that she was able to visibly take notes. That would have been rude, not to mention deeply intrusive, so instead she tried to commit every name, face, and situation to memory.

The new Karlini citizens came from everywhere. There was no rhyme or reason that Saché could determine, except that they had all been enslaved in the Outer Rim and now they were free on Karlinus. She did her best to remember planet names, or at least the systems, while she listened to each person tell their story. Some had been purchased and then freed immediately by an unknown party. Some had been "kidnapped." Some had managed to escape on their own and had fallen in with the newly freed by chance. All of them had arrived on regular civilian transport.

"We were nervous at first, of course," said a Mon Calamari male. "This planet is obviously a center of production, but Xeebi and the others helped us understand that we're only here if we want to be, and that we can take our credits and go whenever we wish."

"You're citizens," Kelma said firmly.

"It takes some getting used to," said Xeebi.

"I don't know exactly how you suffered," Saché said. She pulled down the collar of her tunic, revealing more of the scars that covered her whole body. "But I can sympathize with you a little bit, I think. I still have nightmares. I know it's not as easy as just moving on."

The Mon Calamari nodded and drank his tea.

"I think I've figured it out," Tepoh said some hours later, after plotting every planet name that Saché could remember on a galactic map.

"Well, we're out of caf, so your timing is excellent," Saché said. She was starting to feel jittery, but she knew she wouldn't sleep well with a puzzle to solve.

It was almost midnight, and they'd been at work since Saché had come back to the city.

"It's the front," Tepoh said. Zhe projected the map off the table zhe was working on so that it floated in the air between zher and Saché in three dimensions. "Or some of it, anyway."

"You're right," Saché commended zher. "All of those planets have had Separatist incursions and a Republic Army response. The common thread is they're Outer Rim planets where the Separatists have tried to establish a foothold, places where Republic law doesn't reach."

"But the supply corporations do," Tepoh said. "Not the major ones. Those are focused on the Mid Rim and the Core. But the smaller companies, the ones that used to be merchants and had to repurpose for the war. They don't have the same legislative protection, but they're still trying to make a profit."

"There's no profit in freeing enslaved people," Saché said. "Not in credits anyway. Morally, it's wonderful, but it's a bit uncharacteristic, don't you think?"

"Maybe someone's been waiting for an opportunity," Tepoh said. "I'm not complaining, and I don't think Governor Kelma is, either."

"I'm certainly not upset about it," Saché said. "Just a little bit perplexed. It goes against, well, you remember the Occupation. I'm not used to thinking well of corporations."

"They can't all be terrible," Tepoh said. "The Jedi have a rule or something about balance."

"I'm pretty sure that's not how it works," Saché said. "But as you said, I will take it."

Tepoh yawned, zher face splitting wide, and Saché sent zher to bed. Before she could retire for the night herself, Saché sent two messages. The first was to Sabé directly, to let her know that the work she started on Tatooine had continued, even if she was unaware of the scope. The second went to Sabé, as well, but more formally, to be shared with Padmé as a matter of interest to the sector that Sabé was being told about as a courtesy.

"Someone high up in a corporation is working outside of what we'd expect from something like the Trade Federation's normal operating procedure," she summed up in her recording. "I don't know any of the details, but it is something to consider. We may have an ally. Or it might be a trap. Or it might be a coincidence. But it is unusual, and I thought you would like to look into it if you had the chance."

With the message sent, Saché fired off one more quick
holo to Yané, passing along her love for the kids, and then
she went to sit in the garden. She was tired, yes, but there was
much to think about.

CHAPTER 15

The *Namrelllew* was an old ship, but being of Wookiee construction and design, it was very well built. The air-filtration systems in particular were noticeably superior to anything Naboo could manufacture. There were no particulates in the recycled air at all, and it somehow almost smelled fresh. Padmé quickly decided it was her favorite part of their new accommodations.

The rest of the ship was strangely luxurious, if a bit unusual for humans. Though they had been warned that their cabins would be cramped, Padmé's berth was hilariously long. She was able to keep her entire suitcase at the end of her bed, freeing up the limited floor space. Captain Typho, who had the cabin across from hers, reported that it was larger than any barracks he'd ever lived in, and perhaps the Wookiees were on to something. The refreshers had full-body hot-air dryers instead of towels, and Padmé needed a stool to reach the back of the sink.

The mission to Hebekrr Minor wasn't going to be uncomfortable. At least, not until the espionage parts of it heated up. The *Namrelllew* was much more livable than the shuttle Padmé and Typho had taken to rendezvous with it. They'd stopped at Kebro station to take on more passengers and finally disembarked at Emoh terminus, where they met up with the merchant vessel that was going to be their home for the duration of the trip.

Although the ship was Wookiee-owned, there were only two on board. The pilot, Naijoh, and his wife, Rayyne, who was the navigator. Both understood Basic, and the ship's protocol droid, an aging bipedal unit designated G-1FY, took care of the rest. The fourth member of the permanent crew was the engineer. Padmé didn't meet her at the beginning of the voyage, and then almost tripped over her the following afternoon in the mess.

"Oh, I'm so sorry," Padmé said. She'd gotten so used to looking up for things at Wookiee height, she'd forgotten to look down, too.

"It's all right," chirped the engineer. She spoke Basic with short, high-pitched syllables but was easy to understand. "Must be the new guard."

"I'm half of it," Padmé replied. "My partner is inventorying our cargo."

"Droid for that," said the engineer. "But guards must guard. Must check first."

"Something like that," Padmé said. The mission was clandestine, after all. They would both prefer it if there weren't any surprises in those crates. "My name is Padmé."

"Idda," said the engineer. She turned to look at the table where the afternoon's rations were laid out.

Idda was a Mriss and rarely left the engine room except for food. She was incredibly small, and Padmé wondered how she managed to reach anything on the Wookiee-sized ship. As she watched, the diminutive engineer acrobatically climbed onto the table, selected the food she wanted, and then gracefully descended holding her tray in one hand and a can of meiloorun juice in her beak. She was wearing coveralls that restrained her wings, presumably for safety. Padmé's keen eye for design spotted what she thought was probably the coveralls' escape hatch. Mriss didn't fly, but they did use their wings for balance. If Idda needed hers, she could free them quickly.

"Will you join me for lunch?" Padmé asked, gesturing to an empty seat.

"Eat at work," Idda said. She cocked her head to the side, and Padmé thought this might be what smiling looked like when a person didn't have lips. "Guard come, too?"

"I would like that," Padmé said. There weren't assigned shifts for the guards yet, except a general request that one of them be awake at all times. This meant Padmé spent a lot of time alone, and while she did crave solitude, she knew from previous experience that too much would be unbearable in fairly short order.

She gathered up her meal. Only one of the packages was open, so it was easy enough to be tidy about it. She followed the Mriss through the door of the mess and down a corridor to the engine room hatch. Idda opened the hatch and descended using the same technique she'd used to get her lunch in the first place. Manipulating the large pieces of equipment was no problem at all for her. Padmé was slightly more awkward, stretching between the rungs on the ladder and trying to balance her tray in her free hand.

"Practice makes perfect," crowed Idda, giving an avian laugh. Padmé was not offended. She was well aware that she looked ridiculous.

They ate in relative silence. Every now and then, Idda would look up, click her beak in frustration, and disappear into the engine parts for a few minutes. Padmé could not detect any of the problems the Mriss could, but every time Idda came back down, she had some new grease mark on her coveralls, and she looked pleased with herself.

"Wookiee ships like life. Small moves," Idda explained after the fourth or fifth interruption of her meal. "Good, but work."

"Have you always worked on the *Namrelllew*?" Padmé asked.

"No, Mriss ship first," Idda said. "Too much noise."

The engine was cacophonous, so Padmé could only assume Idda meant the crew, not the ship. She understood that well enough. Sometimes the Senate was so noisy she could hardly hear herself think. The ship, at least, made noise with a purpose.

Padmé finished her lunch and reluctantly took her leave of the engine room. Her only job, until they were on a planet somewhere, was to stay alert when it was her turn to be on shift. The ship could not come under attack in space. Still, she had never been one for idleness, and she respected other people's work too much to distract them at it. She took Idda's tray and rubbish along with hers back to the mess. By the time she was halfway up the ladder, she could hear Idda singing to herself, half in Basic and half in chirps. It was an unreasonably upbeat song about a family of large predatory fish, and she found herself on the edge of laughing again. Sometimes it was good to get away from the Senate.

Typho was in the mess when she arrived, loading up a tray with his own midday meal. She disposed of her trays and took the seat across from him.

"Well, Captain?" she asked.

They were using their own names, more or less, and technically mercenary guards had captains, too. Getting Typho to drop the "my lady" had been more of a challenge.

"Fairly basic medical supplies, for the most part," he said. He opened the package containing his protein ration and made a face. Wookiees had very strong stomachs, and while their food was technically human-safe, its consistency left a bit to be desired in ration form. Padmé tended to drink most of her protein, but Typho preferred something he could chew. "Nothing too surprising or valuable."

"Medical supplies are usually only valuable when they're needed the most," Padmé said. No bacta or spice was a relief. She could fight with a blaster, and had, but it wasn't her preferred method of contact. With lower-target cargo, they stood less chance of being attacked by serious threats. Padmé was fairly sure she could talk her way around anyone desperate enough to steal bandages and antiseptic.

"That's true enough," he agreed. "We're also carrying large quantities of Raadan shurgrain, Karlini tea, and Chadian rum."

That was unusual. The galaxy was new to large-scale war, and Padmé wasn't entirely surprised to find unexpected cargo on board. Maybe someone just needed to get rid of it and had jumped at the opportunity the *Namrelllew* offered.

"The shurgrain I understand," Padmé said. "It helps balance out the digestive systems of most carbon-based humanoids if their water source has been fouled. That could be useful if the fighting gets close to the cities or the planet's main watershed. But what is the rest for?"

"The rum is legal," Typho said. "Though its potential uses on the black market are obvious. Maybe it's a local custom for the people on Hebekrr Minor. No need to interrupt everything because of the war. Sometimes normalcy helps."

He opened the vegetable portion of his rations and ate it with considerably more gusto than the protein.

"I can definitely understand that," Padmé said. "The

Senate is relatively peaceful most of the time, and I still like it when I get some sense of home."

"The tea is the strange part," Typho said. "Karlinus exports it all over the place, of course, but usually to the Core Worlds, or to Naboo itself. Do you remember hearing anything about an increase in production or trade?"

"No," Padmé said. "But I'll admit I have been focused on galactic matters lately, not domestic ones. We can ask about it when we get back."

Typho nodded, washing down his rations with a can of something Padmé hadn't seen the label of. The door to the mess opened, and the protocol droid walked in.

"Greetings," he said. "My captains trust that you are settling in?"

"Yes, thank you," said Typho. Since he was technically the commanding officer, he did most of the speaking for them. It helped Padmé disappear, which made her feel safer without Sabé or one of the others to back her up.

"Wonderful," G-1FY said. "My captains ask that you join them for dinner this evening. It will be on the flight deck, and thus not a formal affair at all, but it will not be rations, so I suppose that's something."

The droid sounded deeply wounded at the idea of not being able to serve them a formal dinner. C-3PO was the same way, though since arriving on Coruscant, his chances had increased rather dramatically. It was strangely reassuring to know that protocol droids had similar problems, no matter where they came from or where they worked.

"We would be delighted," Typho said.

"Excellent," G-1FY said. "I will add the time to your personal schedules. Please be prompt, as the little gremlin who works in the engine room has terrible manners and will not be convinced to wait for you, should you be late."

"Engine gremlin?" said Typho as G-1FY departed.

"A Mriss called Idda," Padmé said. "I actually just had lunch with her, and she seemed delightful, but she did get up and tune the engine a lot. I can just imagine what she'll be like on the flight deck. It's a good thing droids can't have pulmonary attacks."

Typho laughed and launched into a description of the recent time he and Dormé had gone out for a fancy dinner on Naboo, only to be victimized by Eirtaé's wicked sense of humor and a few well-timed explosions.

"I knew it was going to be art," Typho said. "I just didn't realize we were going to be part of it."

"I can only imagine what Gee-One would have thought of it," Padmé said. She hadn't even heard that Eirtaé had an exhibition. The last she knew, her former handmaiden was still working on grain yields and algae blooms. It was nice to know she was able to explore her artistic hobbies, even if Padmé was behind the times hearing about it.

"Dormé swore like a pirate," Typho said. "She had the

nerve to be mad at *me* for not warning her, when I was clearly just as surprised as she was."

"Did you ruin her dress?" Padmé asked.

"Of course not," Typho said. "She can get out stains and cover up singe marks better than anyone in the galaxy. I think she just doesn't like surprises."

Padmé knew from personal experience that was more or less the truth.

"Well, hopefully she won't hold a grudge for too long," Padmé said. "Because there's a new restaurant near the Senate that's supposed to have Hyellian musical noodles, and I think she'd like that."

"Noted," Typho said. "Now, if you don't mind, I'd like to get some rest before whenever it is we're meant to have dinner."

"Of course, Captain," Padmé said. "Sleep well."

Left alone again, Padmé decided that as soon as this mission was over, she would reach out to her friends on Naboo. She'd missed them on her last two trips home and would love to hear what they were getting up to. Moreover, she missed Anakin. When she got back to Coruscant, she was going to prioritize setting up a method of communicating with him. The war was new, but it had already shown her that sometimes you had to *make* the time.

CHAPTER 16

Senator Amidala's new household organization meant that Sabé slept alone. Ellé and Moteé rarely came into her sleeping chamber, preferring to work out of her home office. Dormé moved back and forth between the two worlds, of course, but even she seemed less inclined to linger. The handmaidens who were charged with dressing the senator and caring for her wardrobe and other domestic accoutrement were brilliant, discreet, and ultimately invisible after Sabé dismissed them for the night. She knew that half a dozen people were just a shout away, should she require someone, but after a day of endlessly circular talks in the Senate, Sabé took a moment to savor the quiet.

She'd never had to be Padmé for this long, nor had she ever voted in her friend's name before. Appointing a proxy voter was not uncommon in the Senate, and Padmé had officially made Sabé her proxy in case their deception was uncovered. No one would be able to question the legitimacy of her votes. But Sabé still felt wildly out of place. Padmé had much more influence than she'd realized, was expected to speak and to listen frequently, and was often called upon for advice. It should have made Sabé feel busy and vital and necessary, but instead she just felt tired and overextended. Even with Bail doing his best to cover for her, she felt that her cracks were beginning to show.

She was lonely. Even with so many people around her, clamoring for her attention, she was alone. Without the close bonds to her handmaidens, without the daily dinners with her security personnel, Sabé felt adrift. She didn't understand how Padmé did it, or why things had changed. At first, she had thought Padmé merely wanted some time to herself in the evenings, but this was more than privacy or time for self-reflection. This was isolation. And since Padmé had chosen it, Sabé had to keep it up.

She could read or watch the newscast, but after spending most of her day, every day, debating the war, the last thing she wanted was to hear more about it. She could stare out over the bright lights of Coruscant, except that only reminded her how isolated she was, and how much she disliked it here. She could, if she was desperate, go out to a museum or to the opera. She wouldn't even have to be Amidala when she did it. She was sure Mariek Panaka would help her organize it and see to her safety. Yet there was no indication that Padmé had any interest in that sort of thing, either. She had blocked off all this time, and Sabé had no idea what it was for.

So she sulked. That was really the only thing that could be said about it. She wasn't particularly proud of it, but it kept her from climbing the walls out of frustration and boredom, so she did it.

Tonight, however, she did not have the opportunity. Bail Organa was hosting a soiree, and she had been invited. Only Dormé would accompany her, giving Ellé and Moteé some much-needed time off. Mariek would be their driver.

"That's fine with me," the guard captain said when Sabé tried to apologize for not getting her an invitation. "Senator Organa always makes sure to send the good food to the outside security, and I don't have to pretend I like small talk."

Sabé was a little jealous.

Dormé came in an hour before they were due to depart to help her with her hair. Sabé had done the makeup herself, though Dormé was welcome to make any changes she liked to it, but she couldn't do a senatorial evening hairstyle on her own. The other handmaidens were given the night off, since Sabé could put herself to bed when she got home. As she sat at Amidala's vanity and Dormé pulled the comb through her hair, Sabé took several deep breaths and reminded herself that she had chosen this life a long time ago and had never once regretted it.

"Is there anyone I need to avoid politically?" she asked as Dormé set the comb down and began to twist up her hair.

"No," Dormé said. "This is a loyalist party, so everyone there is an ally. Onaconda Farr has been a little strange lately, but we're not worried about it yet, so you can continue to tread carefully around him."

"Will the Chancellor be there?" Sabé asked.

"I don't know," Dormé said. "He's on the invite list, but he rarely goes to these things when Bail is hosting them. There's a bit of . . . tension there, though for all intents and purposes, they are on the same side."

"I had noticed that," Sabé said. She winced as Dormé pulled a twist particularly tight. "Bail more and more frequently takes issue with the actions of the Republic Army, but he never says anything in public."

"He's very good at waiting," Dormé said. "Senator Amidala often follows his lead to temper her own impulsiveness."

"I like how you can say all that with a straight face," Sabé said, grinning.

"I had a good teacher," Dormé said. "Stop moving your head. I have to set these combs in straight."

With all her hair twisted up and coiled at the back of her neck, Sabé could only move her head in a few directions. This would have worried her, given she would only have one companion for the evening, except she'd already seen the headpiece Dormé planned to use. It was one of Eirtaé's designs, modified heavily by Rabé, and included clever little mirrors that allowed the wearer to see what was happening all around her, even directly behind. It would give the *look* of limiting Sabé's view, but in truth it multiplied it.

Once the piece was in place and Sabé had adjusted her eyes to the additional stimuli, she stood up and walked to the center of the room. Dormé helped her step into the dress, pulling it up over the knee-length deep blue undertunic she was already wearing.

The dress was the palest of pale blues. Sabé held her arms out so Dormé could tie the sleeves. A knot at her shoulder, one just above her elbow, and one at her wrist secured the wide drape of fabric to her arms while some quick lacing on each side fitted the dress to her body. Deep blue cording caught the dress at her waist and formed a delicate bodice that Dormé stuck in place using pins Cordé had designed: invisible and entirely secure.

"These are very clever," Sabé said, running a finger lightly along the line of blue. "I just saw you put them in, and I can't even find them."

"Cordé's whole family was very talented," Dormé said. Her voice caught.

"It's never quite the same, is it?" Sabé mused. "Your separation from your fellows was cruel, but I think I understand a little bit about how you miss them. I'm sorry, for what it's worth."

"Thank you," Dormé said. "You have risked the most of any of us, so it's actually worth quite a bit. I was terrified when it was just me, and off she went by herself with that Jedi. At least I had Typho."

"And I'm very glad I have you," Sabé said.

Mariek appeared in the doorway and nodded sharply at them.

"If you are nearly ready, Senator, it's time," she said.

"Thank you, Captain," Sabé said. "Dormé?"

"We are ready, my lady," Dormé said. She would do a final check of Sabé's dress when they arrived. She pulled her navy hood up over her head.

"Lead on, Captain," Sabé said.

Mariek huffed a laugh at her tone but said nothing further as she escorted them down to the transportation platform and into their vehicle. The drive to Senator Organa's apartment was mercifully short, and before long Senator Amidala was making her grand entrance to his party.

The gathering was on the roof of the building where the senator lived. It was protected from the high winds at this altitude by large glass slabs that had scenes of Alderaanian mountains etched into them. Everywhere Sabé looked there were Alderaanian plants and pieces of art that incorporated wind or water. It must have cost a fortune, but then Alderaan had been a member of the Galactic Republic for a very long time.

"Senator, I'm so glad you could join us!" Bail said when he saw her. As usual, no one looked at Dormé.

"Of course, Senator Organa," Amidala replied. "Your invitations are always the best received."

She moved down the receiving line, greeting the few Alderaanian dignitaries and artists who had been invited. Then there was nothing for it: she had to mingle. Sabé quickly located Mon Mothma in the crowd and made her way over. The tall red-haired human was one of Padmé's closest allies—though not one of her closest friends—in the Senate. It was a distinction that Sabé found frustrating, but it appeared to work for both of them.

"Senator," Mon Mothma said. She nodded regally. Whatever Mon Mothma had been about to add to her greeting was cut short by the arrival of a new person to their assembled group.

"Senator Amidala, how wonderful to see you out and about," said Chancellor Palpatine. "You have been almost cloistered lately. I know you take the war as seriously as any of us, but it is good to see you taking some time to yourself with your friends and colleagues. Try the Toniray. Senator Organa has a particularly good vintage available tonight."

Sabé took the glass he passed to her and raised it in a silent toast before taking a sip. It was sweeter than the alcohol she'd been getting used to on Tatooine. And probably less likely to eat through her gut while she was digesting it. She suddenly missed Tonra so powerfully it made her stomach hurt. She hoped he was doing all right.

"Thank you, Chancellor," Amidala said. "It is difficult to stop working under these circumstances, but Senator Organa reminds me that everyone needs a rest sometime."

"Good, good, I'm glad to hear it," Palpatine said. "And I think, my dear, you'll be glad to hear my news, as well. A few Jedi of your acquaintance are back on Coruscant for debriefings and reassessment. I had hoped they would be here tonight, but I suppose we shall have to look forward to other gatherings in the coming days."

Sabé blinked at him and took a sip of her wine to cover her hesitation. It was an amateur move, and he surely noticed it, but she couldn't think of anything else to do on the spot. Dormé was behind her. She was on her own.

"That is good news indeed," Amidala said. "The Jedi are new to sustained war, as well. They deserve a rest as much as we do."

"Indeed." Palpatine narrowed his eyes slightly. Whatever he had expected to get from her, he hadn't gotten it. Her lack of reaction had given her away and he now had only additional questions. This was exactly the sort of scrutiny Amidala didn't need right now.

She was saved by one of the performers from the Alderaanian opera, who came over to ask what she thought of the most recent season. This was, at least, something she could talk her way through, since she genuinely enjoyed both the subject matter and talking to artists about their work.

It wasn't a spectacular victory of an evening, but it was a good showing, and by the end of it, after two more glasses of the Toniray (which was, actually, very good), Sabé was feeling more relaxed than she had since she'd arrived on Coruscant. Her discussion with Palpatine almost forgotten, she was even willing to admit she'd had a good time, though Mariek did her the courtesy of not asking her about it on the ride home.

Alone in her room in the senator's apartment, Sabé took the ornaments out of her hair and combed it until the coils were mostly smooth again. She cleaned her face and pulled off the undertunic so she could put on the nightgown Dormé had left out for her when she'd put the blue dress back in the wardrobe. She drank a glass of water and then refilled the cup so she would have it on hand when she woke up, and tucked herself into Padmé's comfortable bed.

She was almost asleep, warm and still a bit fuzzy around the edges, when she heard a noise like a door opening and shutting, and then the soft footsteps of someone who knew what they were doing crossing the antechamber outside of where she slept. She fought to stay still, to look like she was sleeping, and reached for the blaster that lay under her pillow.

There was someone in the doorway of her room.

CHAPTER 17

Padmé usually spent at least an hour getting ready for an informal gathering, so it was something of a vacation to pause only long enough to rebraid her hair before striking out for the flight deck. She was punctual, which she knew because Typho opened his door approximately half a second after she did, and he was always on time for everything. She hoped Idda wouldn't be too impatient with them.

As they made their way through the ship, Padmé seriously considered looking into buying a Wookiee ship to be her official senatorial conveyance when she got back to Coruscant. Sure, the Naboo ships were comfortable and familiar, but the *Namrelllew* never made her feel claustrophobic, even when she was in a small room. Wookiee design was good for that, but there were many species in the galaxy who would probably be more at ease on a ship like this instead of one designed for humans, no matter how good the craftsmanship was. If she was going to do a lot of missions to the front lines, it might be worth checking into.

Their arrival on the bridge interrupted her musing. The

control center of the *Namrelllew* was relatively self-contained, mostly because it was crewed by only two people. The bridge had a narrow—for Wookiees, presumably—corridor at the rear where the nonflight controls were, and then a protruding flight deck that bubbled up out of the hull. In hyperspace, the view was mesmerizing, but Padmé had no fear of getting lost in it. There was too much going on.

Naijoh and Rayyne, as cocaptains, usually had front-facing chairs. Since it was dinnertime, the chairs were turned around, looking away from the controls and back into the ship itself. A table was suspended above the floor, lowered from a cleverly concealed hatch in the wall. Idda was perched on the end where the table attached to the wall, and G-1FY stood at the other end, pouring drinks. There were two empty chairs, and Padmé and Typho waited politely.

"Please, take a seat," Rayyne said via the protocol droid. Her gestures made her statement clear enough, but G-1FY was something of a chronic repeater.

As Padmé and Typho settled in, Typho making sure that Padmé was not on his blind side, G-1FY passed them each a cup of tea and then slid one all the way down the table to Idda.

"Iffy, juice!" the little avian said. Naijoh rumbled a warning, and without looking the slightest bit abashed, Idda elaborated: "Iffy, juice *please*."

"Karlini tea is known throughout the galaxy as the perfect precursor to a meal," G-1FY said. He sounded even stuffier than C-3PO. "It prepares the stomach and clears the throat for incoming flavor and texture. Juice, in its various forms, is more widely accepted as a drink for breakfast. Or younglings."

Idda sniffed and took a large swallow of her tea. A little bit of steam seemed to come out of her ears.

"Thank you, Gee-One," Padmé said. "Or, is it Iffy?"

"If it must be," the droid said. He sounded resigned to the fact. "Have you had Karlini tea before? Some find it over-spiced, but it is an excellent palate cleanser."

"We are familiar with it," Typho said. It was something of an understatement, but they were undercover.

Padmé took a sip of her tea. It was brewed perfectly, and she missed the entire Chommell sector rather fiercely for a moment.

"Have you done much security since the war began?" asked Naijoh, again speaking through G-1FY.

"A bit," said Typho. "Most of our work together is from before that, but we're no strangers to conflict. The galaxy is a dangerous place, and my partner here seems to attract it."

Padmé glared at him, but both the Wookiees laughed.

It soon became apparent that while the Wookiees had been content to hire security personnel through the company they had contracted with, they wanted to know more about the people who now traveled with them on the *Namrelllew*. Padmé let Typho do most of the talking, and most of the stories he told were true. He left out a great many details, but there were plenty of missions and expeditions Senator Amidala had gone on that had turned out to be completely boring, at least from a security standpoint. It was kind of interesting to hear about her work from his perspective. In the old days, she had known the ins and outs of every procedure that kept her safe, but as her Senate responsibilities grew, she relied more and more on those she trusted. It made her a better senator, but she missed the old closeness.

"I noticed you didn't bring many weapons," Rayyne said to Padmé through the translator droid. G-1FY was dishing out the entrée, some sort of stewed tuber with a pungent orange sauce that promised to be full of flavor, and didn't miss a beat.

"My captain here is better suited to that sort of conflict," Padmé said. "Though I can and have used a variety of blasters. My talents lie more in diplomacy. If I can't talk us out of it, Typho takes over. If he can't shoot us out, well, then it's my turn."

"Our employers decided to go with a small, flexible team and rely on Republic forces out in the field, it seems," Naijoh said. "I can't really blame them. It's definitely cheaper, and we're already charging them a lot for the hauling. It's still early in the war, but I hope we never require large-scale incursion teams just to deliver medical equipment and a few odds and ends."

It was the longest speech Padmé had ever heard a Wookiee

give, and she worked with their senators. It was like listening to music. Sometimes, she felt like she was right on the edge of understanding him, and then the logical part of her brain took over and reminded her that she didn't speak Shyriiwook past basic greetings. They listened to stories from the Wookiees for a while as they ate. Both of them were very well traveled, and not even G-1FY's monotone could take the punch out of their adventures.

Anything they might have discussed after that was halted by Idda's slow, determined campaign to offload her keldrin-peas onto the floor without anyone noticing. Of course, G-1FY wasn't fooled for a moment, even while he was busy serving dessert and translating for Padmé and Typho.

"In some cultures," said the droid, "it is customary not to serve dessert to those who did not properly savor their vegetables."

Idda put a pea on her spoon and fired it straight into his face. It got jammed in the little opening where the droid's mouthpiece was, and he couldn't dislodge it with his blunt fingers. He crushed it instead, which gave him the appearance of having a very strange dimple on one side of his mouth.

"Well, I never," he said as Idda fled back to the engine room, cackling as she went. The Wookiees roared with laughter, and even Padmé had to cover her mouth so as not to hurt the droid's feelings.

"I think you'll have to take that as a draw, Iffy," Typho said, offering up his napkin so the droid could wipe his mouth.

"Thank you, sir," the droid said with great dignity. He set Idda's abandoned dessert down in front of Naijoh. "Sometimes that's all a hardworking droid can expect around here."

"Dinner was wonderful," Padmé said. "Thank you."

"We mostly eat the rations," Rayyne said, G-1FY moving the napkin away from his face to say her words. "But for a special occasion this is good, too."

Padmé volunteered to carry plates back to the mess, and Typho helped G-1FY fold the table away. She made it back to their quarters before he did and waited in the hall for him to return. When he did, he opened the door to his room and welcomed her inside.

"Well, I don't think the Mriss is up to anything," Typho said, settling on the end of his bed. "Except bugging the hell out of that protocol droid."

"Wookiees don't like being taken advantage of," Padmé said. She leaned back against the tall sink. "If someone is cheating them, or using them, both Naijoh and Rayyne could muster their entire families to seek justice or revenge. That's a lot of angry Wookiees."

"One of the reasons I chose this ship is that we didn't think the Wookiees were involved in anything sordid," Typho reminded her. "We knew they worked for the company, but so far, everything with that has checked out, too. If not for the tip to the Jedi and the request for a meeting, this report would never have made it to Senator Organa's desk."

"Well, if it's not the Wookiees and it's not Idda, could the droid be transmitting something?" Padmé asked.

"Maybe," Typho said. "He looks like a normal protocol droid, but there's no way of knowing if his programming has had a boost. He was quite good at multitasking at dinner. But he couldn't be sending images. Just text or sound."

"I'll see if my scanners pick anything up," Padmé said. "I don't have anything general enough to scan the whole ship, but if it's just the droid, I can manage it easily enough. He spends more time in the mess than I do, so finding him is never a problem."

"All right," Typho said. "I'm going to ask for some maps of our landing zone. I want to make sure this handoff goes as smoothly as possible. You should take your rest hours now, if you can. That way we'll both be in awake cycles when we get to Hebekrr."

"Yes, sir, Captain," Padmé said. Typho's skin darkened with a blush.

"For the record, my lady, I do not like being undercover," Typho said. "Or at least, not so far from the rest of our support."

"I don't love it, either," Padmé said. "I guess this is what Sabé feels like all the time, though. It's just her and Tonra. If nothing else, it's adventurous."

"The idea of you having adventures makes my stomach ache," Typho said. "Please just go to bed."

Padmé laughed and followed orders.

ϟϖϖϟ

The droid's intelligence-gathering capacity was exceptionally limited, but he was all that was available to work with, and so worked with he was. G-1FY knew the guards were human. He knew they had come from Coruscant, though they had tried to cover their tracks by hopping around a bit before they joined the *Namrelllew*. He knew they were patient and willing to do all tasks aboard ship. He knew they were hiding something, like so many spacers were. This was very, very good news.

Neimoidian Oje N'deeb had had high hopes when he'd leaked his information to the Jedi those few weeks ago. He gleaned from studying the newscasts that the high-ranking Jedi interacted primarily with a select group of senators, and that one of them was *her*. She was integral to his plans. He needed her for influence and opportunity. And if he was lucky, she was exactly the person who had come.

He couldn't be entirely sure. The droid knew only the guards' species and origin point, and Coruscant had literally billions of people who matched that description. Furthermore, he had seen *her* on the newscast several times, most recently just this evening as the holonet news covered a party thrown by Senator Organa.

Still, if there was anyone who could make it happen, it was her. The pacifist queen who had fought a war to save her planet. The diminutive senator whose failed execution had sparked a galaxy-wide conflict. Wherever she went, it seemed, trouble followed. And he had called, hoping she would answer. Hoping she would come to Hebekrr Minor and see for herself. Because he had plans for the future. For himself and for his company and for Neimoidia. And he needed her for any of those plans to have a chance to succeed.

CHAPTER 18

"Where is Padmé?" a harsh voice demanded.

Sabé was pulled to a sitting position on the bed, the blaster flying out of her grip across the room to crash against the wall. She tried to shout, to raise the alarm, but she couldn't move or make a sound.

"Where is she?" The question was repeated.

The lights came up, revealing a tall figure in a brown Jedi jerkin. His handsome face was crimped with suspicion and barely concealed rage. Sabé gestured to her throat, and the feeling of pressure all around her relaxed.

"Who the hell are you?" Sabé asked as soon as she got her breath back. "And how do you know how to get past all of our security protocols?"

The two of them stared at each other, at an impasse, until C-3PO wandered into the antechamber, the lights turning up to their brightest setting as he entered.

"Master Anakin, it is you!" he declared. "I'm quite pleased to see you again. Did you happen to bring Artoo with you? I imagine the little scoundrel has managed to survive all manner of firefights. Oh, and al—"

"Anakin?" Sabé cut off the rambling droid. "Anakin Skywalker? From Tatooine?"

"That hasn't been my home for a long time," he replied. He relaxed a little bit. Seemingly, C-3PO's acceptance of the situation put him at ease. "You're Sabé, aren't you? The shadow. The one I met."

"Yes," Sabé said. "Padmé called me back here to pose as her while she went on a mission for the Senate."

"Is it dangerous?" Anakin said. It was like he was going to fly out the window in hot pursuit if given the slightest idea that it was necessary. "Is she in danger?"

"No," Sabé said. "Well, not any more than usual. Captain Typho is with her. I assume you know how protective he is."

"Master Anakin, have you had dinner?" C-3PO interjected. "It is late, but I am sure I can arrange for something."

"No, thank you, Threepio," Anakin said. "We can manage on our own for a bit."

His manners were still impeccable, like when he was a little boy, but, Sabé remembered, he was the one who had programmed C-3PO in the first place. Several pieces of the puzzle that was Anakin's presence fitted together neatly in her head.

"You and Padmé," Sabé said.

Anakin bristled, like he was ready for a fight.

"It's none of your business," he said.

"I am in my nightgown, and you are in my room," Sabé said. "I think it's at least part of my business."

"She—" Anakin started. He looked down at his hand, flexing his newly tuned metal fingers inside his glove. "I love her," he said. And then, like it was a dare: "She loves me."

It all made too much sense. Why Padmé had disappeared on Naboo. Why the schedule had changed and why the staff had such a new routine. This was why Padmé's evenings were free. This was why her handmaidens slept on the floor below instead of in the penthouse suite as they used to. She hadn't done it for herself, not to make a separation between her career and her personal space. She had done it all for *him*.

"You're angry," Anakin said. "That doesn't bother me. I'd be angry, too, if she picked you over me."

"That's not how it works, Jedi," Sabé said. "Padmé's heart is infinite, and she loves many, many people. Not to mention her feelings about duty and her job. If you haven't figured that out yet, you will soon enough."

"Maybe," Anakin said. He didn't sound entirely convinced.

Sabé rubbed the bridge of her nose and shivered. She remembered that her nightgown was sleeveless, and that Anakin was letting all the carefully regulated air of her bedroom drift into the antechamber. She'd been having such a lovely night, too.

"Let me find a robe," she said, and paced over to the

wardrobe. She picked one at random, hoping Padmé hadn't worn it too frequently, and went back to the bed to down her glass of water.

"All right," she said. "Since you're clearly not going to leave until I give you a full explanation, here's how it is. Padmé is on a mission for the Senate. I don't know all of the details, and I wouldn't tell you even if I did. She's safe, she's with Typho, and she's doing her job. I am filling in for her because the Senate needs her. She's a reliable figure, and she has many alliances with other factions that her close colleagues do not. Is that enough for you?"

"I guess it'll have to be," Anakin said.

"In that case, may I please go back to bed?" Sabé asked. "Threepio can show you out."

"Uh, about that," Anakin said. "The security override I used resets the system. I can't let myself out for at least three hours. And if you or Threepio do it, it'll show up in the records. So, um, if you wouldn't mind . . ."

"You have got to be kidding me," Sabé said. She had no interest in having a sleepover.

"Jedi can sleep anywhere," Anakin said quickly. His bravado had drained away, and suddenly he was awkward and young again, instead of dark and dangerous. "I'll sleep on the floor in the antechamber, don't worry."

"I have half a mind to make you sleep in the trash

compactor," Sabé said. "But all right. Will you be warm enough? Is that a Jedi thing, too?"

"Yes," Anakin said. "I don't even need pillows."

"Well, you've got some anyway," Sabé said. "You might as well make yourself comfortable."

She watched as Anakin rather half-heartedly built himself a nest on the long sofa. She did not help him. He retrieved his cloak, wrapping it around his body as he sat down. She went to turn out the lights.

"What's it like out there?" she asked, hand hovering above the switch.

"The war?" he said. "It's just fighting. The Separatists have droids and we have clones, and they fight."

"I've fought droids, too, remember," she told him. "I know it's not that simple, even if you have a clone army to back you up."

"It is simple," Anakin said. "The Separatists want to break the galaxy into little pieces, every one of them looking out for their own self-interest. The Republic is peace and justice. We're not invading. We're not forcing worlds to supply us with weapons or food or other resources. We're helping people who are oppressed. Restoring the galaxy to order. Bringing them back to the light."

The way he said it, so convinced of his declaration, it was tempting to believe, but Sabé knew that things were rarely so cut and dried. Padmé certainly didn't believe it. That's why she worked so hard in the Senate. She believed that policy and diplomacy would bring errant systems back into the fold. Sabé was sure of it. This violence that Anakin spoke so glowingly of was terrifying because it felt so easy.

"It's all right if you don't believe me," Anakin said. "You haven't been out there yet, not since the fighting really started. I'm not careless with the clones."

"I'm glad to hear that," Sabé said. "Remember that Padmé is fighting this war, too. She's going to do things differently than you, and she has to act like she's a normal senator. You don't keep secrets very often, and that's how you are, but Padmé's life and work is secrets. Can you respect that?"

"I'm trying," Anakin said. "I like it when everything is straightforward. I trust Padmé, though. I know she's not like most politicians."

"Well, I suppose that's a start." She turned off the light. "Good night, Anakin."

She walked back into her bedroom. He made her uneasy in a way she couldn't explain. His conviction and his dedication to fighting were at odds with the small, sweet boy she remembered meeting, officially, on Naboo. He'd been the only one to ask her name. The only one to thank her. And now he was grown, a Jedi Knight, and connected to Padmé in ways that Sabé feared were deeper than he had admitted to. Maybe she *was* jealous. But she wasn't wrong.

She closed the door, hearing the lock hiss into place with some relief. She filled the water glass a third time and put herself back to bed.

＞◡◡◟

The Jedi was gone when Sabé got up in the morning, and she was glad of it. She was giving a speech in the Senate that afternoon, so it was Dormé who came to dress her for the occasion. For once, Sabé didn't pay attention to the makeup or the hair. She felt like the dress was going to stifle her. For the first time in more than ten years, she didn't want to be Amidala. She wasn't sure if she knew her anymore.

"I had a visitor last night," she said neutrally as Dormé put the finishing touches on her hair and straightened her collar.

"Oh?" Dormé said. And then: "Oh, shit."

"Pretty much," Sabé said. "Are there any other secrets I should know about before they show up in my bedroom after three glasses of Toniray?"

"That's the only one I know of," Dormé said. "I'm so sorry. I thought you knew."

"Padmé didn't tell me," Sabé said shortly.

There was an awful silence between them.

"And . . . are you okay?" In that moment, Dormé's pretences and professionalism dropped away. For a heartbeat, they were two girls who shared a secret with their friend, even though it made them uncomfortable.

"I'm upset to find out the way I did," Sabé said. "But it's not like this is the first time someone has fallen in love with her. This is just the first time she's fallen back. She told me once that if she ever did, it would be complete and consuming, and I guess she was right."

She was angry—and upset—but there was no one here to be angry at, and she hated being upset with Padmé. They would talk about it calmly when Padmé got back. Years ago, after the Harli Jafan incident, they had agreed to talk about any issues that arose between them as soon as possible. And now Sabé had an issue. Sabé stood up and let Dormé do the final check of her dress. It seemed heavier than usual, the edges sharper and the fabric less forgiving. She knew that nothing had really changed since the day before, but the dress felt like it didn't fit.

"I'm going to request to tell Ellé and Moteé, when Padmé returns," Dormé said. "They'll have to know. Padmé is the soul of discretion when it comes to organizing trysts, as I am sure you can imagine, but Anakin is as subtle as a drunken gundark."

"I noticed," Sabé said drily. "I don't envy you."

"Of all the scandals she could have picked," Dormé said. "Of all the scandals she's been accused of!"

Against her better judgment, Sabé started to laugh. It felt

like hysteria, clawing its way out of her throat, and yet she didn't want to stop. For the first time since she'd woken up with Anakin Skywalker at the foot of her bed, she felt almost normal again, like she could be the senator and not be on the brink of failure at every moment. Padmé's humanity made it easier to pretend to be her.

"Padmé's never done anything halfway in her life, and you know it. Why should this be any different?" she said. Then she sobered: "The droid knows. He used to be Anakin's."

"Where do you think Artoo-Detoo went?" Dormé asked.

"Isn't he Naboo government property?" Sabé responded.

"I think that's beside the point," Dormé shrugged. "The droids are reliable. The new handmaidens don't suspect anything. Ellé and Moteé are busy with work at the Senate. Typho will definitely figure out that something is up, but he won't ask. Mariek will figure out exactly what's up but won't confirm or spread gossip."

"I guess that's what happens when you surround yourself with loyal people," Sabé mused. "I wonder how many other senators are so secure with their own households."

"We all know it goes both ways," Dormé said. "And we all know what we signed up for, even if the details are a little different."

"I don't like it," Sabé said. She wasn't sure if she meant Anakin, the new layers of separation in the house, the Senate, the whole war, or everything all at the same time.

"But you'll do it," Dormé said. It wasn't a question, but there was the opportunity to give an answer buried in it.

"Yes," said Sabé. The dress settled a little better on her shoulders, and she marshaled her thoughts toward the speech she was due to give in a few hours. Padmé needed her to be Amidala, so she would be Amidala. For now. Until Padmé came back and they could talk about it, open and free, the way they always did. "Yes, I will."

CHAPTER 19

Hebekrr Minor was, as the name suggested, the second habitable planet in its solar system. Hebekrr Major had been geologically unstable for some time, though people had lived there in the distant past. Occasional expeditions were sent to recover ancient technology and cultural artifacts from the planet's broken surface, but no one could stay there for very long.

The fighting on Hebekrr Minor was centered on the largest population concentration in the planet's southern hemisphere. The Republic Army and the Hebekrr militia held the city, while Separatists made incursions from the surrounding hills and destroyed whatever arable farmland they came across. They hadn't come to Hebekrr for food, after all. The planet's true wealth lay in the minerals that laced its soil. If the Separatists couldn't make a profit from them, no one would. The only small mercy was that the planet wasn't exactly a Separatist priority, so there was very little air support, and no ships had been left behind.

The *Namrelllew* slid into orbit in the empty sky above the

planet's surface. Padmé and Typho joined the Wookiees on the flight deck so they could scan the landing area for themselves.

"There's no space inside the city's fortifications for a ship of this size," Typho said. "But we expected that would be the case. Padmé and I will take the shuttle, make the supply run, and then return here. Will either of you be coming with us?"

Naijoh shook his head and trilled a negative. It wasn't so much that the Wookiees trusted their security as it was that Padmé and Typho had nowhere to go. And also they wouldn't get paid.

"All right then, Captain," Padmé said. "Let's go load up."

G-1FY helped them with the cargo sleds as they loaded the shuttle. The little ship had minimal shielding and one forward-facing gun, but it would do. They did not expect heavy fire, and the clone troopers knew they were coming, so they would be able to provide ground defense. It took only a few minutes to finish loading, and then they were ready to be away.

"Shuttle One departing," Typho said into the comm.

The bay doors opened, and even though Padmé was in a sealed vessel, she still imagined she could feel the cold pull of depressurized space.

"Affirmative," said G-1FY. "The captains tell me to wish you good flying."

"Thank you," Padmé said. "We'll meet you at the rendez-vous point when we're done."

Typho piloted the ship out of the bay, and then they began their descent toward the planet. As expected, the clone communications officer picked them up almost immediately and provided them with safe landing coordinates, and an evasive route to avoid any of the Separatists' heavy guns. They landed without incident, and unloading proceeded quickly.

"Cee-Cee-Seventeen-Seventy-One, clone commander, reporting," said a trooper with thin blue stripes painted up and down the arms of his armor plating. "Everything seems in order. I have your boss's credits ready to send."

Padmé could not resist asking a few questions. It might be the only chance she had to interact with clones at the front.

"What do you call yourself, Commander?" she asked.

"Sticks," he replied. She wished she could see his face but wasn't sure if it was polite to ask him to remove his helmet. She knew what he looked like, of course, but there was a lot to be said for eye contact.

"Nice to meet you, Commander Sticks," Padmé said. "Is there anything else we can do for you while we're here?"

The commander seemed to hesitate, leaning forward on the balls of his feet before possibly remembering that, for all he knew, she was merely an independent contractor, not a senator to whom he owed anything at all.

"If you have some time to wait, I would ask that you speak with my general," Sticks said at last. "General Sivad and his apprentice are at the magistrate's house, and they may require your aid, if you can give it."

"Of course," Padmé said, just as Typho returned to her side. She felt him wanting to protest, but he said nothing. "Please, Commander, lead the way."

Sticks issued a few more orders, including that the shuttle be refueled, and then escorted them through the city.

"Are you sure this is a good idea?" Typho whispered. "It's a deviation from the mission."

"It's a deviation from our primary mission," Padmé said. "But this is the first chance someone from the Senate has had to see how the front lines operate. We've been relying on Jedi reports, which are adequate, but occasionally they overlook things."

"Just try to keep it under control," Typho said.

"Of course, Captain," Padmé said.

The city must have been a pretty place, once, but constant barrage and siege living was starting to take its toll. Many of the windows were blacked out or boarded over, the shops were closed, the parks were empty, and the plant life was wilting.

"We've been under siege here for several weeks," Sticks told them as they walked. "Almost since the very beginning of the war. The Separatists tried to buy mineral rights, and when the local government refused, they tried to take them. That's when we stepped in. Now, the clankers seem focused on destruction, hoping the magistrate will crack."

"Do you think she will?" Padmé asked.

"That's not for me to say," Sticks said. "Though there are other factors in play that General Sivad will explain."

They arrived at the magistrate's house and were admitted immediately after Commander Sticks vouched for them. Even here, signs of the siege were readily apparent. The house was reinforced structurally and was serving as a back-up hospital for anyone with non-emergency issues. They were also operating a soup kitchen out of the state dining room. Everything was organized, but there was a tinge of desperation in the air. The people here were very close to breaking.

Sticks led them into the command center, a large meeting room in the middle of the house. It was, Padmé guessed, usually where public meetings were held, but the clones had repurposed it quite efficiently. Sticks brought them to the Jedi and waited to be acknowledged.

"General, Magistrate," Sticks said. "These are supply pilots. They just dropped off more medical supplies and various other items. They have their own ship and are technically not affiliated with either side in this conflict."

"Very good, Commander," General Sivad said. He was a short, stocky human male with white-blond hair and a florid, friendly face. "Magistrate, the Force has given us a chance to reset the balance here."

The magistrate of Hebekrr was a human female at least seventy years old. Her face and hands were both lined and cracked, signs that she had worked just as hard as any of her constituents before she turned to politics. When she looked at Typho and Padmé, a great weight seemed to lift off her shoulders.

"The Separatist army has been demanding a meeting with me," she said. "They are not subtle. They'll clearly make me sign something if they get anywhere near me. Our best recourse so far has been to draw the siege out. They'll have to run out of droids eventually, and the mineral rights on Hebekrr aren't worth that much."

"We've fortified the city as best we can," General Sivad added. "We all agreed that protecting the magistrate was the priority, so she has stayed in this house."

"All of that was working until ten hours ago, when a group of organic Separatist agents breached the defenses of a farmhold two hundred kilometers east of here and kidnapped my granddaughter, her wife, and all three of my great-grandchildren." The magistrate took a deep breath. "We have been stalling for time ever since, but obviously any objectivity I had is long gone."

"Usually, I would step in as the neutral party," General Sivad said. "But with the Council's decision to take sides in the war, that is no longer possible. Both I and my Padawan would be considered enemy combatants."

"My men have put together an extraction plan," Sticks said. "But without a neutral vessel, our intent would be quite obvious."

Padmé looked down at the map of the besieged city and the surrounding area. It was not unlike parts of Naboo, though obviously Theed's geomorphology was more dramatic. She couldn't just go back to Coruscant and give a cold report of what the front was like. As a senator, Padmé had to help, even if they could never know that she was, in fact, very strongly affiliated with their side. As a person, Padmé saw no question at all. It was Queen Jamillia's sister again, where political capital must be considered as additional weight in a game of numbers, however unfair it was to everyone else.

"All right," she said. "I think I have an idea."

Beside her, Typho sighed. He knew exactly where this was going, but the truth was, he wouldn't stop her even if he could. This was what Padmé did, and he had known that full well when he'd signed up to be in her service.

"How badly did you want that Chadian rum?"

They loaded the rum, Commander Sticks, and six other clones in stealth armor onto the shuttle. It was a tight squeeze. Then they took off and set orbit above the city. When they were absolutely sure the Separatists had had enough time to scan them, Typho opened a comm channel.

"This is *Namrelllew* resupply shuttle calling the Separatist base," Typho said. "We're unaffiliated with either party and have supplies on board, if you are interested in purchasing them."

There was a long silence, and then an organic voice spoke.

"This is the Separatist quartermaster," he said. "We know you just came from the city landing pad."

"Yeah, and they didn't buy all of our cargo." Typho sounded deeply annoyed. "Do you think I want to haul it all the way back to my boss and then have to explain why I didn't even try to sell it?"

"We are mostly a droid army," the quartermaster said. "We have very few needs."

"It's Chadian rum," Typho said. "No one needs it, but it's nice to have around, you know? I'll give you a better deal than I was going to give those Republic cheapskates."

There was another long pause.

"We are showing a high number of life signs on your vessel," the quartermaster said.

"Well there is a war on!" Typho said. "I'm not going to travel around without security. Look, are you interested or not? I'm burning fuel, here."

"Very well," said the quartermaster. "Land at these coordinates. Open your shuttle's hatch. Do not disembark."

The comm went silent.

"Is that enough?" Padmé asked.

"Oh, yes," Commander Sticks said. He sounded excited. Padmé could understand. War was ugly, but he'd been made for it. She knew what it was like to have a job that felt like pure fire when it was going well.

Padmé went to the weapon case on the wall of the flight deck and took out her blaster. Typho carried his on him, but she preferred the small vibroblade Dormé had designed to fit in the sleeve of the pilot's tunic. Now she was going to need a gun. It wasn't the delicate silver blaster that Queen Amidala had used, and neither was it the bulky E-5 blaster rifle that Senator Amidala had used during the arena fight on Geonosis, but it would do the job. She clipped the blaster and several extra power cells onto her belt and then took her seat next to Typho. In the back, she could hear the clones doing the final checks of their own weaponry and gear. It was reassuring, in a way. These were soldiers, and they were very good at their job. She trusted them, and not just because she'd seen them in action before. They exuded an aura of competency.

"Take us in, Captain," Padmé said.

She forgot that, technically, she wasn't giving orders on this mission, but no one questioned her. Typho brought the shuttle back down to Hebekrr's surface, and Padmé Amidala stepped into the center of galactic conflict once again.

CHAPTER 20

The problem with most of the people who lived on Naboo was that, barring a weeklong period of extreme hardship more than a decade ago, very few of them had any idea what true suffering was. They were brimming with empathy and good intentions, but they had very little in the way of practical experience. If anything, their collective trauma gave them tremendous potential to act badly: it was possible that in an effort to avoid repeating the events of the Occupation, they would take measures without considering the effect on neighboring planets.

Saché was determined to avoid that, but her colleagues back on Naboo were not making her job any easier. By flatly refusing to cancel the legislation that offended the other Chommell sector planets so much, they had forced Saché into a defensive position she didn't even agree with. She would have much rather started over from scratch, but Governor Bibble had tied her hands: it was amendments or nothing, and it had better not be nothing.

Governor Kelma was, at least, the perfect choice of mediator for the negotiations. Karlinus was the wealthiest planet in the sector, after Naboo itself, and yet it was still trusted by the outlying systems. Even Harli Jafan listened to her, which was helpful, because she certainly didn't listen to anyone else.

"What's to stop Naboo from just throwing all this out the moment it becomes inconvenient for them?" Harli asked several hours into discussion of the current draft. She'd stopped pacing a while ago, and now she just gestured from her chair, occasionally thumping the table for emphasis. "There is nothing here that holds Naboo accountable."

"If you can't trust us to hold ourselves accountable, how can you trust any legislation at all?" Saché asked. She was starting to get a bit frustrated, even though she understood Harli's reluctance. Still, if there wasn't any trust in the foundation, how would they be expected to build anything? "There has to be some measure of meeting in the middle, Representative Jafan. That's what compromise is."

"It's not much of a compromise if the only change is that Naboo benefits a little bit less," Harli said. There was a murmur of agreement from the other delegates, most of whom were in attendance holographically.

Saché pinched the bridge of her nose. She didn't even disagree. She hated arguing for a position she wasn't entirely on board with, though she was a professional and she understood what was at stake. The Chommell sector had to hold together as the war went on. Naboo couldn't stand on its own, and it couldn't ruthlessly pillage the surrounding planets to survive. The only way to solve the problem was to coalesce into something stronger than a single planet or system, and then hope like hell that everyone held up their end of the bargain when it came to sacrifice.

"What if we change the terms of the power flow, a little bit," Saché said. It was an idea that had been hovering in the back of her mind for a couple of hours now, and this was the time to voice it.

"What do you mean?" Kelma asked. It was the first time the governor had spoken in a while, other than to control who had the floor.

"Right now, Naboo only requires two of its three legislative bodies to agree on any major policy change. Some combination of the queen, the governor, and the legislature itself." Saché tapped the table in front of her. "What if it was all three of them? In a blind vote, simultaneously?"

"You mean, everyone would vote on their conscience, and if there was any dissent, nothing would happen?" Harli asked. "You'd never get anything done ever again."

"We'd have to fine-tune it, obviously, and I was thinking it would be specific to this arrangement, and this arrangement only," Saché said. "We could rewrite the language so that only combined authority of Naboo has any sway. And that almost never happens. At the very least, the queen would refuse, and if she had the power to veto, more representatives might vote . . . bravely."

"Ah, Naboo idealism," said one of the holograms. "It's nice to know some things never change."

Saché inclined her head and let them laugh at her expense for a moment. She could take the hit to her ego, and she was sure it would pay off anyway.

"It'll have to be really specific language," Harli said. She leaned back in her chair and stretched. Saché knew that she'd won. "Some sort of . . . sector-wide power alignment that viewed Naboo as a single entity that had to agree with itself internally."

"We can start working on it as soon as you like," Saché said. She tapped open a new draft of the legislation on her datapad.

"Oh, you're not getting off that easy," Harli said. A wide grin split her face. She was clearly back in good spirits. "There are other terms I want to see changed."

"I am not surprised in the slightest, Representative Jafan," Saché said. She could afford to be gracious: she'd already gotten what she was after, and now it was just a matter of hammering out the details. "Shall we get to work?"

The economics were the most complicated part. They spent almost a full day arguing over the difference between fair market value and fixed prices, and which would benefit whom more. Saché mostly sat that part out, unless Tepoh flagged something for her attention. She didn't really care what the bill ended up saying. Her job was to codify who controlled it when it was done. Also, she genuinely didn't know what the going price of unprocessed denta beans was.

The resulting document was a far more equitable give-and-take among all of the planets in the Chommell sector. Naboo could expect to face some shortages in terms of food production and the cost of construction material the longer the war dragged on, but it wouldn't be insurmountable, and it was no more than any other planet was asked to give up. There were definitely some issues with the power grid, if outside laborers from Jafan stayed home as the bill suggested, but that was an internal matter, and Naboo would deal with it.

"Let's never do this again," Harli said quietly to Saché as the hologram of Governor Bibble and Queen Jamillia appeared in the meeting chamber to hear the final draft.

"It's a deal," Saché said. "From now on, it's capers only, nothing substantive."

"Thank you for doing this," Harli said. "I know you only agree with about half of what you argued for. It means a lot that you would stake your reputation for us. We don't vote for you, and your people are the ones who might end up shorted."

"Putting Naboo first has never gone well for Naboo," Saché said. "In the long term, anyway. I like to think I am better at the long game."

"Oh, definitely." Harli indicated Governor Bibble with her chin. "When you've got his job, we're going to have an absolute blast."

Saché made an indelicate sound into her hand and then forced her attention back to the historic event taking place in front of her. All of the planetary leaders and delegates of the Chommell sector agreed to the amendments on the bill without further debate or clarification. The signing took place quickly and without ceremony, on account of those who had been tirelessly debating for days. Finally, it was done. Saché was clapped on the shoulder by everyone present, and someone handed her a glass of sparkling wine to celebrate. She toasted Governor Kelma silently from across the room and then drained her cup with Harli.

Tepoh appeared at her side about fifteen minutes into the celebration, zher ever-present datapad in zher hand.

"I took the liberty of having all of our things packed up," zhe said. "There's a late shuttle run back to Naboo tonight, if you wanted to catch it?"

"I really do," Saché said. "How much time do I have?"

"About thirty minutes," Tepoh said. "I'll have everything sent on ahead."

Saché shook hands with Harli and then fought through the crowd to get to Kelma's side.

"Thank you again for hosting, Governor," Saché said. "If you don't mind, I'd like to duck out and head home."

"Of course, my friend," Kelma said. "Tell Yané I said hello."

Saché smiled and took her leave. Before she knew it, she was back on the shuttle bound for Naboo. Home was a little bit safer now. A little bit better. And soon it would be very, very close.

⟆⟇⟇⟆

He had wondered what they would do with the dilemma he placed them in. It was a thought experiment in many ways for him. A tooka cat amongst pigeons. An amusing sideshow while the bigger pieces of the galaxy aligned themselves to his will. Naboo had always been his testing ground, after all. There was no reason to change his methods this late in his machinations.

Bringing the original bill to the attention of Quarsh Panaka had only been the first link in a chain he couldn't see the end of. Or, rather, he could see several ends and wasn't sure which they would pick to follow. All of them would benefit him, though. Eventually. That was the only game he played.

The Naboo legislature had reacted exactly as he had expected. They remembered being hungry, herded into camps.

They wouldn't want to experience that again. Representative Saché had reacted exactly as he'd expected, too, with her bleeding heart and her determined good nature. She'd gone straight to Karlinus and set up sector-wide talks.

He honestly wasn't sure what would have been more amusing: the sector falling apart and turning on each other or the sector coming together, like a giant rock that would take slightly longer for the ocean to erode.

Their solution had surprised him. Oh, he didn't care about the details. The rise and fall of the agricultural market didn't interest him on a practical level, and he had no stake in construction on backwater planets like Jafan. What interested him was that Naboo had chosen to weaken itself. Not only in terms of resources, which they could always just purchase outright if push came to shove, but in political power.

The whole planet, queen, governor, and legislature had to act as one if the bill was ever to be overturned. It was a precedent-setting decision, and he could hardly believe that Saché had gotten everyone to agree to it. But Queen Jamillia was Padmé Amidala's protégé, and Governor Bibble was her puppet in so many ways, and the legislature nearly hung itself trying to keep her on the throne. It might have gone better for them if they had. As it stood, there was a weak point in the power structure that even Saché had not considered, because it was so unthinkable to Naboo's functionality. They had always been a triumvirate: elected queen, elected representatives, appointed governor from that body. They never imagined that someday the very essence of how Naboo was ruled would change.

How fortunate that, in the future he planned, Sheev Palpatine had only one leader for Naboo in mind.

CHAPTER 21

Commander Sticks took point in the operation immediately, issuing orders to the troopers. Smoke bombs and other confusion-spreading incendiary devices preceded them down the ramp. Small pulse bombs were targeted at the droids. Padmé and Typho wore their helmets so the gases wouldn't affect them. The Separatists weren't caught entirely unawares. A well-timed delivery during a hostage crisis wasn't the most subtle play in the book, but they had underestimated the amount of firepower that well-trained clones could pack into a small space. The clones overwhelmed the droids that met them on the landing dock, and then paused to regroup once the zone was clear.

"Our intelligence indicates that the magistrate's family are being held in that building," Sticks said. "Stay here and dump the rum while we extract them."

"Understood," Typho said. If he thought he had any chance of making Padmé stay inside the shuttle, he would have pressed the issue, but he knew enough to pick his battles.

The clones set out. The measured fire of the blasters, punctuated by the occasional larger explosion, spoke of discipline and training. This wasn't like the arena fight, which had been a little bit desperate, waves of clones attacking as an overwhelming force. This was a precision strike, and even though the war was only a few weeks old, the clones were already experts at fighting it.

A second wave of enemy droids rolled into the landing bay just as Padmé steered the final sled into its position. There were only three of them, two battle droids and a destroyer, but that was more than enough. Padmé shouted a warning to Typho and dove behind the crates of rum. The cases would withstand the blaster fire, so she wasn't worried about an explosion. Being outflanked was another matter.

"Please tell me you have a vibroblade sewn into your sleeve," Typho said from his position, pinned on the ramp. The ship's gun was facing in the wrong direction.

"You think Dormé ever lets me leave the house without one?" Padmé replied.

"I'm going to draw their fire and take out the battle droids," Typho said. "Get behind that destroyer and stab it in the processor."

It was, without question, the most dangerous thing he had ever suggested that she do. And she was ready to move without a single hesitation.

"Good to go!" she called back.

Typho gave a loud bellow and plunged down the ramp.

He bore left as soon as he reached the bottom, drawing the droids' attention away from where Padmé was crouched. He shot the battle droids as he ran, and the destroyer followed his movements, spinning slowly on its gimbal.

Padmé waited as long as she could and then took off toward the destroyer at a run. The ground was slippery from spilled grease and general untidiness, but she wasn't worried about losing her footing. She turned the grease to her advantage, sliding feetfirst under the destroyer's carriage. Even at a run, she was slow enough to pass through the shielding. Before the destroyer could re-aim its weapons, she plunged the vibro-blade into its processor core. The spidery droid shorted out, and she stabbed it a few more times for good measure until it lurched sideways in a shower of sparks and came down on top of her.

"My lady!" Typho was at her side in a flash, pulling metal in every direction in a frantic effort to get it off of her. It took a moment, but between the two of them, she was able to wiggle free.

"I'm all right, Captain," she said, looking him right in the face. She knew they were both thinking about Cordé, burnt and dying on the Coruscant landing pad.

"I thought—" he said. "I remembered."

"I know," she said. "I'm fine. We're both fine. And I am not in a hurry to do that again."

There was a massive explosion from the rear of the compound, and then Commander Sticks came on the comm channel.

"Shuttle One, Shuttle One, we need an extraction." The comm buzzed. "Shuttle One, can you come and get us?"

"We're on our way," Typho said.

He pulled Padmé up the ramp and into her seat on the flight deck. Her legs had started to shake. Whatever confidence she'd felt in the heat of the moment was waning now. She forced herself to focus. They weren't done yet. She'd barely finished strapping herself in when Typho took off, not bothering to retract the ramp. A quick hop in the air took them over the burning building, and they saw the clones easily in the light of the fire. All five of their targets were with them.

Typho brought the ship down, hovering above the ground as the clones got the rescued prisoners and themselves up the ramp. Padmé could hear the clank of approaching feet. They were running out of time.

"Go! Go!" came Commander Sticks's order from the back.

Typho pulled up sharply, the metal screaming as the ramp tried to close in spite of the torque working against it, and then they were safely away.

"Let's not do that again in a hurry, either," said Padmé, her heart racing.

"Agreed," Typho said. His hands still gripped the controls too tightly.

"I'm going to make sure everyone's okay," Padmé said.

"We should be back to the magistrate's house in fifteen minutes," Typho said. "It's a straight flight."

Padmé clasped his shoulder as she walked past him. He finally let go of the controls to reach up and squeeze her hand. The last time they'd been on a secret mission together, there had been a body count. They didn't talk about it, at least not with each other, but the specters of Cordé, Versé, and the others had loomed large in their minds. The demons would never be fully exorcized. They would always wonder what they could have done differently, how they might have saved their friends.

But this mission was a success. They hadn't let fear incapacitate them. They had trusted each other. And they had gotten the job done. Now it was just a short hop to get these people home, and then it was on to the next.

The scene at the magistrate's house was quietly jubilant when Padmé returned with Typho and the rest of their party. The makeshift hospital and charity food kitchen still marked the siege, but the atmosphere had changed. Hope had been restored. It was quite unlike the stiff formality and vague reluctance with which Jamillia and Antraya had greeted each other when Padmé and Anakin reunited them. But it was no less important, politically speaking, than that mission had been.

Padmé watched the magistrate hug her granddaughter and granddaughter-in-law, and then pull all the children close to her. She knew they were talking to each other, but she couldn't bring herself to eavesdrop. She knew better than most what a person might say in the heat of a dangerous or emotional moment.

"Thank you," said Jedi Master Sivad, appearing at Padmé's side with a small Ithorian Padmé took to be his Padawan. "The Jedi walk a difficult path at this time, and I am glad to know that you are walking it with us."

He was so calm that Padmé legitimately could not tell if he recognized her or not. She didn't know him, but the Jedi had a way of sharing information she wasn't privy to. She decided not to press the issue. It served all of their purposes better if her cover remained intact, even with those she might have otherwise befriended.

"Yes, thank you both," the magistrate said. "We took up a collection to pay you for the rescue. We don't have a lot of Republic credits, but—"

"No," Typho said before Padmé could intervene. "Rescuing people for money is not something I do. It's not something we do."

"Will you stay here, now?" Padmé asked. "Keep your family close so that this doesn't happen again?"

"We took out the clankers' armory and their recharging stations," Commander Sticks reported. "I don't know how many battle droids they have left, but even with solar backups, they'll run out of power before long. Maybe a week at most. We can definitely hold them for that long."

"But what happens after that?" Padmé said. "Your company would be assigned somewhere else, correct?"

"That is true," said General Sivad. "This posting was not meant to be permanent."

"I suppose," said the magistrate slowly, "that we could join the Republic."

She didn't sound very enthusiastic about it. The others in the room made noises expressing vague distrust and outright refutation. It was a good solution, and the only one Padmé could see, but even with her feelings about the galaxy being better off united, this wasn't how she liked to win recruits.

"I can—" she began, and Typho coughed. "I know a guy," she corrected. "It'll be basic groundwork only, but it'll buy you some time and you'll be entitled to full Republic protection even during the preliminary talks."

The Jedi looked at her closely but didn't say anything. That was definitely not something a common mercenary would know or be able to promise, and he knew it. He nodded at her and put his hand on his Padawan's shoulder.

"Very well," said the magistrate. "We will open negotiations."

"And it is my honor to protect you in the name of the Republic," said Commander Sticks.

"Can you stay?" asked one of the children they'd saved. All three of them stared at Typho like he was the most interesting person they'd ever seen. Adults were sometimes put off by his eye patch, but children were never afraid of him, which Padmé knew amused Dormé immensely.

"I'm afraid not," he said. "We're already overdue back at our ship."

Commander Sticks and the Jedi escorted them back to the shuttle, leaving the magistrate some time alone with her family.

"I suspect all is not entirely as it seems," Commander Sticks said by way of farewell when they reached the docking bay. "But you're clearly on the right side of this, and I hope our paths cross again."

"Good luck, Commander," Padmé said. She inclined her head slightly in the direction of the Jedi. "Master."

"May the Force be with you," Sivad said.

The bay door closed, and Typho took the ship gently back into space. Padmé was really looking forward to relaxing back on the *Namrelllew*. Her pilot suit was comfortable, but it was not designed for sliding across docking bay floors, and she felt like she was covered in grease.

"It's never going to end, is it?" Typho said. It wasn't really a question, but Padmé respected him enough to give an answer.

"No," she said. "It never does. The combatants change, and I would understand if you wanted to stop fighting and go back to Naboo to get married, or take up orchid farming, or whatever. But this? Doing what's right for people who can't? That never ends."

"I can only speak for myself," he said. "But I'll stay with you as long as you need me."

"Thank you, Captain," Padmé said.

The *Namrelllew* came into view in front of them, and Typho signaled that they were ready to dock. The doors slid open to welcome them, and Typho brought the shuttle in for a safe landing.

Idda was waiting for them, bouncing on her little feet and ready to do any maintenance the shuttle might require.

"Carbon score?" she said accusingly when she saw the small marks the shuttle had picked up during the rescue. "Drop only, and carbon score?"

"It got a little bit complicated," Typho said. "That's why your captains hired us to take care of the delivery instead of asking you to do it."

That answer did not mollify Idda in the slightest. She chirped at him in her own dialect, and Padmé didn't need a protocol droid to know she was using scandalous language.

"I'll help you clean it up," Padmé said, hoping that would calm the little avian down.

"No, no," said Idda. "Shuttle mine. You go get clean."

She turned back to her work, already singing that song about the fish again. It was more than a little catchy. Padmé was never going to get it out of her head at this rate. Escape was the only option.

"I'll make our report to the Wookiees," Typho said. "Hopefully I run into Iffy on my way to the flight deck."

"Thank you, Captain," Padmé said. "I really do feel kind of gross."

She went to her cabin and put the outer layers of her pilot uniform through the cleaner while she washed the grease off of her skin. It was impossible to get truly clean without a full shower, but at least this way Padmé felt better. She could wait until her ration time came up to do the rest.

She pulled the tunic and trousers back on when they were dry and fastened the belt. She wanted to sleep now that her adrenaline was wearing off, but something told her she couldn't. They still hadn't met the contact who'd tipped off the Jedi Council. Their time on board was almost done.

She opened the door to go check on Typho and found G-1FY standing there waiting for her.

"Senator," the droid said. Her breath caught. "If you'll come with me."

CHAPTER 22

The Jedi generals had been spread thin at the outset of the war, and many of them were recalled to the Temple for assessment and reassignment. Chancellor Palpatine wished to take advantage of the number of Jedi who had returned to Coruscant by having them meet with Senate members. Since a party was not suited to Jedi taste and the Senate schedule was already full of daily meetings, it was decided that a group of senators would make a pilgrimage to the Jedi Temple itself. Senator Amidala was, naturally, amongst those selected to attend.

Sabé was not looking forward to seeing Anakin Skywalker again. He made her uncomfortable, and he almost certainly was capable of forgetting himself and blowing her cover. Master Kenobi was also a threat, although a lesser one: she'd fooled him before, and he was less likely to announce her secrets in public.

It ended up not being much of a problem. Rather than formal talks, the Jedi seemed to prefer a softer approach to military debriefing. The senators were taken to one of the Temple gardens, and there they circulated among the assembled Jedi and Padawans, asking questions of whomever they liked. It was easy for Sabé to avoid the Jedi she didn't wish to talk to and seek out conversation that was more appealing.

"Master Billaba, I am glad to see you looking so well," Amidala greeted her old ally. Sabé had flown with her once, but as far as Depa Billaba knew, she had spent more time with Padmé on the Bromlarch mission. "It is good to see a Jedi who was spared the fight on Geonosis."

"I did not escape the fighting for long," Depa Billaba replied. "But that battle was particularly nasty. It is thanks to the special attention of Padawan Barriss Offee that those who were injured recovered so well I think."

The Padawan in question drifted toward them at the mention of her name, and Sabé did not have to reveal that she didn't know who the girl was.

"Padawan," she said by way of hello. "You were on Geonosis, too, correct? I'm sorry to be so vague. It's a bit of a blur."

"I was," said Barriss. "With Master Unduli."

"And have you been in battle again since then?" Sabé asked.

"No," Barriss said. "I am not afraid to fight, but I do not want to fight in a war."

"That is a wise answer," Sabé said. "It's the sort of thing I like to hear from a Jedi."

The girl shifted uncomfortably, her gaze sliding to Billaba in the absence of her own master.

"It's all right, Padawan," Depa said. "The senators have come to hear our opinions."

"I will avoid fighting as long as I can," Offee said. Her eyes met Sabé's directly. "My master has trained me to fight, and I am good at it, but I prefer to work in the medical center. The arena on Geonosis was a lot to deal with and I am not too proud to admit that I was scared."

"I don't think that's a bad thing," Sabé said. "If we need Jedi to fight, we need them to heal just as much."

"Afterward, I had trouble sleeping," Barriss continued. "Several were injured, and I volunteered to watch the Temple clinic at night, even though it's not really necessary."

"Is there nothing Jedi can do after a battle to recover?" Sabé asked.

"Many meditate," Barriss said. "But my head was too noisy. I couldn't focus. Some of us recover by going down to the younglings' levels, where the youngest Jedi learn and train. We find it soothing to teach the children or to listen to them play."

"But you didn't?" Sabé asked.

"No, Senator." Barriss looked at Depa again, but the Jedi Master did not intervene. "It was hard. I am not very much older than some of them. The Masters had come down to watch them train, and they were so excited at the idea of being chosen as Padawans. I wanted to tell them that war is nothing to get excited about, that it's awful and that they are too young, but the Jedi have been made the generals of this war, and we must serve."

"I was fourteen when I fought for my planet," Sabé said. "But that was over quickly."

"And it still did damage," Barriss said.

"Yes," Sabé said. "Many of my friends have scars, visible and otherwise."

"They deserve better," Barriss said. "All those younglings deserve better than what I saw out there."

"They do," Sabé said. "And I think your feelings make you the perfect person to make sure they get it."

"There may come a time when we are called to go against our nature," said Master Billaba. "When that comes, we must be open to possibilities."

"I will be, Master," Barriss said.

Sabé didn't think that was exactly the sort of comfort the Padawan needed, but it wasn't her place to intervene. Barriss seemed troubled, unsure of what she should be doing. Sabé could understand the feeling. She didn't feel suited for war, either, or at least not the sort of war that was being fought in the upper levels of Coruscant. And she had the freedom to leave, eventually. Barriss Offee was a Jedi, and that wasn't an easy thing to leave. Though, she knew, there was at least one Jedi who flouted the rules. She hoped Barriss would find balance and a way to serve. She hoped the same thing for herself.

She let Master Billaba guide her over to where a Jedi Master named Plo Koon was holding court, discussing the tactics his clone trooper squad, the Wolfpack, employed.

"The more individuality the clones show, the better the unit functions," Plo Koon said. "It's contrary to what the Kaminoans told us, but it's undeniably true."

"Agree with you, I do," said Master Yoda. "Individuals, they are, and treat them as such, we must."

An enormous Jedi with a vaguely reptilian face made a derogatory noise but said nothing. Very few people, even Jedi Masters, argued with Yoda.

"Senator Amidala." Anakin Skywalker appeared at her elbow. Sabé glared daggers at him, but he pretended not to notice. "I have some information about the Mid Rim, if you would like to hear it."

It was a laughably weak excuse, but no one commented on it. Sabé went with him to the spot in the garden where a dozen miniature trees basked in the sun. She was fuming silently. She was here to gain knowledge, not run messages between her friend and the impetuous Jedi.

"I wanted to apologize for how I treated you the other night, at Padmé's apartment," Anakin said. Sabé was pleasantly surprised. She hadn't expected an apology, and it was clear from his face that he'd put some thought into it. "I was surprised and more than a little disappointed, and I reacted badly."

"Thank you," she said. "I accept your apology."

Anakin laughed ruefully, and for the first time, Sabé saw shadows in his face of the little boy he had been. He was quite good-looking, now that he was grown-up.

"I know we'll never be friends, exactly," he continued. "But we both care about her a lot. You risked your life for her more than once, and you'd do it again. You protect her differently than I would, and in ways that I can't. Could we at least declare a truce?"

And he was charming, too. There was an odd sincerity to him that Sabé knew right away was the real reason Padmé had fallen for him. Whatever else you could say about Anakin Skywalker, he might just be the most genuine man in the whole galaxy.

"Truce," she said. "And thank you for protecting her when I can't."

"It's what I signed up for," Anakin said. He put his hands behind his back and grinned at her, unabashed and honest.

The truth of everything hit Sabé all at once.

"She married you," she said. "It's not an affair. It's a permanent relationship."

Instantly, Anakin was on the defensive again, their truce evaporating at the first test.

"She makes her own choices," Anakin said. "You know that."

He stalked off into the Temple, blowing past Master Kenobi when he tried to get him to talk to Bail. Sabé barely watched him go. She threw up every wall she had, every trick and technique to conceal her emotions and hold herself together in public, while inside she was reeling. Padmé did make her own choices, but this was something huge, and she had done it without involving Sabé at *all*. It made her feel vulnerable and superfluous, and Sabé didn't enjoy the feeling.

"Is Jedi Skywalker all right?" Chancellor Palpatine asked, appearing out of nowhere and looking concerned.

"Yes," Sabé said, hating him for making her cover for him. "He just remembered he had a teaching appointment. With the lightsabers."

It wasn't her best work, but the Chancellor didn't seem to care.

"Walk with me?" He extended his arm, and she had no choice but to take it.

"Of course," she said, and placed her hand lightly on his sleeve. The fabric should have been familiar, like home, but Palpatine had long since given up wearing Naboo-made clothes. The difference was entirely shallow, but Sabé felt it anyway.

When you walked with the Chancellor, people got out of your way. It was subtle, but it was true, nonetheless. Sabé didn't like the way they deferred to him. It seemed strangely out of place, like they were moving before their minds were made up to do it. He was a government official worthy of respect, of course, but they were all public servants here.

"We're at the beginning of momentous times, I'm afraid, my dear," Palpatine said as they walked. Sabé knew—undeniably—that the Chancellor knew exactly who he was speaking to. "Everything is going to change. Chaos will claw at the door, and it is up to the Senate to keep that door closed."

Sabé knew that already. She'd lived it when Naboo was occupied, and she'd done her best to stem the tide working on Tatooine. What politicians on Coruscant saw as a faraway interruption or a procedural hiccup, she had experience first-hand. There was still sand in her boots to prove it. Palpatine could say whatever he wanted, but it wasn't on Coruscant that the work would get done.

"I'm going to rely on you even more in the coming days, Senator," Palpatine said. This was a message, too. If she stayed, there would be many more days like this. "Your steady presence here in the Senate chambers reminds me of what we're fighting for, of what we're trying to achieve."

It was too much. Between her revelation about the nature of Padmé's relationship with Anakin and the patronizing way the Chancellor was looking at her, Sabé felt like there were walls closing in around her. Darkness pulled her down, and despair welled up in her soul for a reason she couldn't quite identify. She fought it off. It was an uncomfortable weight on her chest, but she did her best to dislodge it.

"Thank you, Chancellor," she said, her voice carefully level. It was almost the Queen's voice, something she hadn't used in years. "I do my best."

"I couldn't do this without you, my dear," Palpatine said. He smiled avuncularly at her and patted her on the hand. It was extremely irritating. "I'll let you get back to the Jedi."

He left her by a little pool in the Temple garden. The trickling water helped her control her breathing. The sparkling light on the water's surface drew her imagination to brighter things. The darkness and despair were gone, but she remembered what they'd felt like all too well.

"My lady?" Moteé came over to see how she was.

"Just a little lightheaded," Sabé said. "I skipped lunch again."

Moteé knew very well that she had done no such thing but understood the signal clear as sunlight.

"Do you want to go?" Moteé asked. She had at least a dozen excuses at the ready, should something be required. Amidala's handmaidens were always, always ready.

"No," said Sabé after a moment. "There is much to be learned here. I just need a moment."

Moteé nodded and stayed with her until Sabé felt ready to go back into the crowd. The strange feeling had completely passed now, and it didn't look like anyone else was affected. Maybe it was Anakin's discomfort projecting itself onto her or some trick of Temple magic. Sabé knew the Force was limited, after a fact, but she had only a rough idea of what it could do. Surely here, in the Jedi center on Coruscant, there were bound to be little blips of rogue power from time to time.

Only it had seemed so dark, and the Jedi were meant to represent the light. Regardless, Sabé now knew with absolute certainty that her time on Coruscant was coming to an end. When Padmé returned, they would have a talk, but Sabé had no idea what would happen next. It terrified her more than the darkness had, that yawning chasm of unknown in her future.

Sabé looked back at the little pool and felt her center come again to balance. She could not stay here, not even for Padmé. And she hadn't the slightest clue how she was going to break the news to the best friend she'd ever had.

$$\text{✶ ✦ ✦ ✶}$$

Senator Amidala was indisposed for only a short period of time. Aside from her ever-present handmaiden, only one other person in the garden had noticed. He watched her as she moved back into the crowd, listening to each Jedi as they told stories about working with the clones, and what fighting the Separatists was like. She listened attentively and asked intelligent, insightful questions, as everyone expected that she would. She gave no indication that mere moments ago, she'd felt anything strange at all.

He wasn't surprised that she'd shrugged it off almost immediately, of course. Most people did. But the feelings lingered in ways that weren't always noticeable. Ways that could be exploited later. The seed of the idea had already been there: the doubt and insecurity. He had merely waited for the perfect timing, and then ensured that certain forces made it grow.

Chancellor Palpatine watched Senator Amidala circulate through the crowd, his expression as blandly polite as apioc pudding. Only the slightest upward twitch of his mouth gave him away, and no one was looking at him for long enough to see it.

The water in the sparkling little pool dried up, and no matter what the Jedi's groundskeepers did, they could never fill it again.

CHAPTER 23

Padmé followed G-1FY down the corridor because she didn't really have a choice in the matter. She hadn't even had time to stitch the vibroblade back into her sleeve. She could overpower the droid easily enough, unless he electrocuted her, but she knew she couldn't take either of the Wookiees without a weapon. G-1FY didn't lead her toward the flight deck, though. Instead, he took her to a little room across from the mess. The sign on the door read MAINTENANCE, and Padmé had never needed to go in.

"If you don't mind, Senator," G-1FY said politely.

"Why do you call me that?" she asked, more to stall than anything else.

"Because that is your title," G-1FY said. "I only learned that recently though. I cannot believe that the captains made me serve you such a wretched dinner with that little menace at the end of the table throwing peas at me. The indignity!"

"I very much enjoyed your cooking," Padmé said honestly. It wasn't the droid's fault that it could be reprogrammed.

"Oh, that is so nice of you to say," G-1FY said. "I—but I am getting distracted. If you will please go in here, there is someone who wants to talk to you. I promise you will be quite safe."

Padmé didn't have a lot of options. She knew the room had to be pretty small, even by Wookiee standards. If it came to close-contact fighting, she wasn't the strongest, but she also was unafraid to fight dirty.

"All right," she said. She drew herself up straight and, for the first time since she'd left Coruscant, drew the full mantle of Senator Amidala about her. "Open the door, Iffy."

On the other side of the door was the dim blue glow of a hologram. That was some measure of safety then. A hologram couldn't do her any physical damage. Padmé stepped into the room, and G-1FY shut the door behind her. As her eyes adjusted, the figure's shape and species became clear.

"Ah, Senator Amidala," said a drawling Neimoidian voice. "I was hoping it would be you."

Typho couldn't get his door to open. Now that he had given his report and cleaned up, all he wanted was a ration pack from the mess and a nap in his berth, and the door was jammed. The control panel responded, the lock would activate, but the door wouldn't budge. Not even throwing his shoulder against it a few times did any good. He had just started to look around for his blaster when the comm system in his room activated.

"Captain Typho, please do not distress yourself," said G-1FY. "My employer required a few moments to speak with the senator alone, and so I have sealed your room for the next while. I recommend beginning your rest period early."

Typho's mind homed in on the most important word the droid had said, and he felt panic rise.

" 'Senator'?" he demanded. He threw his shoulder against the door again. It didn't move.

"Oh, dear," said G-1FY. "Yes, my employer is aware of your identity and so am I. I assure you she is quite safe. It is merely a holo."

"Then why have you locked me in here?" Typho punctuated the sentence by kicking the door as hard as he could. Still nothing.

"I assumed you would react poorly," the droid said. "I do not think I was incorrect."

"I'll show you incorrect," Typho blustered.

Whatever G-1FY might have said next was drowned out by the sound of screaming metal. Typho flinched away from the door as sparks flew, and then the whole thing fell inward to reveal Idda, clinging to the doorjamb with a welding torch in her hands and giggling somewhat maniacally. She'd gone right through the metal and circumvented the droid's seal.

"Captain, please," G-1FY appeared down the hallway. "I promise you, everything is fine."

"Locking me up really doesn't inspire my faith in you,

droid," Typho said. He looked down at Idda, who had climbed back to the deck. "Thank you, little one."

Idda stuck her considerably long tongue out at G-1FY and made a rude buzzing noise. Then she looked at Typho and held up her arms to him. Typho picked her up and put her on his shoulder. Then he strode down the corridor, pushing the droid out of the way when he feebly tried to block them.

"Do you know where she is?" Typho asked.

"Near mess," said Idda. "Other door."

Typho set off as quickly as he could with G-1FY spluttering behind him.

"What do you want, Neimoidian?" Padmé asked. She was surprised at the venom in her voice. It had been ten years since the Occupation, but there had been several threats to her life since then, and the Trade Federation had been at the center of them all. She bore scars on her back and abdomen from their most recent attempt, and Nute Gunray had cheered gleefully while it happened.

"Just a conversation," the Neimoidian said. He held his hands up beside his face, his fingers spread wide. "That's why we're talking via hologram. I am not anywhere close to you right now. I pose no threat. I merely wish to explain myself."

Padmé took a deep breath and marshaled her thoughts.

She had *known* that whoever the informant was would make contact eventually. She just hadn't been prepared for this. She owed it to the Senate to be better. She owed it to herself.

"I will hear you," she said. Her voice was once again formal and polite.

"That is all I ask," the Neimoidian said. He took a last moment to prepare his thoughts, and then he began.

"My name is Oje N'deeb. I believe we just missed one another on Nooroyo not too long ago," he said. "I am the largest stakeholder in a company that controls, well, much of the trade in the Outer Rim right now. The legal trade, anyway. The Syndicates and the rest of the Trade Federation have not let the war slow them down."

"I imagine not," Padmé said.

"I represent a group of my people who seek to repair the damage that our fellows have done," N'deeb continued. "We didn't actively participate in the blockade on your planet ten years ago, though we did nothing to stop it, and we haven't engaged in any weapons or manufacturing trade since. Our interests are purely agricultural and medical, mostly low-value goods that don't make enough profit to interest anyone with criminal tendencies."

"And then the war broke out, and you found yourself sitting on one of the most important trade routes in the Outer Rim," Padmé surmised. She knew how quickly the tables could turn.

"Correct, Senator." N'deeb blinked several times. "Unlike my competitors, we have not up-marked any of our trade goods. We have focused on selling to planets and systems that are sympathetic to the Republic or are under attack by Separatist forces. The most recent venture to Hebekrr is typical of what we do now."

"Out of the kindness of your heart?" Padmé asked, an uncharacteristic cynicism creeping into her tone.

"Not entirely, of course," N'deeb said. "Credits do add up, and our investments are so low-risk that we almost never lose money. More importantly, we wanted to prove to the Senate, and to you specifically, that we were serious."

"Serious about what?" Padmé asked.

"We want to replace Lott Dod in the Senate with one of our own people," N'deeb said. Padmé's mind spun at the thought of it. "It won't be me. I have too many skeletons in my closet, even for a Neimoidian. But we want our people to be represented by someone . . . well, by someone else."

"A sympathetic Trade Federation would bolster the Republic significantly," Padmé said. The possibilities were endless. "And the damage to the Separatist cause would be immeasurable."

"We know," N'deeb said. "Our chief issue is first convincing the Senate that we are serious, and then taking care of our internal problems."

"That's why you needed me," Padmé said. "Of any senator

in the galaxy, if you could get me on your side, your chances would increase dramatically."

"Precisely," he said. "And do we have you?"

It would be beyond foolish to turn him down outright. At the very least, Padmé should present the idea to her faction. Bail would jump at the opportunity, and Mon Mothma would like that they didn't trade in arms. Padmé expected that her personal prejudices would flare, make her suspicious or petty, but despite her initial reaction, she felt nothing. This was another piece on the board, another move that could gain the Republic an advantage in the war. She could do this.

"Why Karlini tea?" she asked. It was a missing piece in the puzzle of N'deeb's motivations.

If N'deeb was thrown by the segue, he gave no sign of it.

"There were some amongst us who thought that aiding your system's economy would help," he said delicately.

"Well." Padmé almost laughed. "I am sure Governor Kelma appreciates it."

"My droid informs me your guard is on the way," N'deeb said. "I will leave you to do the complicated explanations. Iffy has my contact information when you are ready with an answer."

"Thank you," Padmé said. "For trying to be better."

"Sometimes it's the only thing you have left to do," N'deeb said. He was very solemn when he said it, and Padmé believed him.

His image flickered out, plunging the room into total darkness. There was the sound of fists hammering on the door.

"Padmé?" Typho yelled.

"I'm fine!" she called out. She hauled the door open and looked up at him. With Idda perched on his shoulder it was hard to take him seriously. "I'm fine, Typho."

"I'm still going to kill that droid," Typho growled.

"Dis-mem-ber-ment!" Idda chanted, biting off each syllable with great enthusiasm. "Dis-mem-ber-ment!"

"Leave Iffy alone," Padmé chided them gently. "He's only the messenger, and I needed to hear the message very much."

"Oh?" Typho said. With both Idda and G-1FY in hearing range, he couldn't be more specific.

"I'll tell you later," Padmé said.

"Fair enough," Typho said. "This one and I are headed back to the flight deck, then. We have to tell the captains about some, uh, property damage."

The sound of Idda's cackling echoed in the corridors.

✶✶✶✶

Back in her room, stretched out on her ridiculously long berth, Padmé shuffled all of the thoughts in her head. The fighting on the Outer Rim was vicious and personal. The Separatists struck hard against defenseless people, and the Republic was going to be hard pressed to fight them everywhere. The army of droids, soulless and expendable, was going to keep coming unless they found a way to disrupt supply lines and the flow of credits into Trade Federation coffers. The solution that Oje N'deeb offered seemed like an impossible dream, yet it was real. And it was worth fighting for.

She would explain the reality of the situation to him. They were looking at a lot of concerted effort. Possibly years, depending on how the fighting went. She didn't think N'deeb had any illusions, but she wanted to be honest with him. Her battle in the Senate would be no less laborious. The Trade Federation did not have the best reputation with Republic loyalists, and it would take more than a few humanitarian trade routes to convince them otherwise. Padmé's reputation was strong, but the war was stretching her thin.

She needed to talk to Sabé as soon as possible. Sabé was much more practical than she was and would probably see a clearer path than Padmé, so used to getting mired in procedure, would. It was good that they were headed back to Coruscant. The Wookiees were going to take them the whole way and look for cargo in the capital to take back to the Outer Rim. Soon Padmé would be home. She had learned a lot, seen a lot, out here. But it was time for her to get back to work.

Once there was a girl who watched a planet die while she tried to save it, and she swore she would never stop trying.

She had accompanied her father on the aid mission despite the protests from some of the senior organizers. They argued that she was too young. She was only nine at the time, but she had a good head on her shoulders, her father countered, and she was interested in the work. It was never too early to foster that sort of generous spirit. So they had taken her with them, to a planet with a dying sun.

The girl was immensely popular amongst the refugees. She was kind and she was approachable. She made friends easily, and many of the adolescents could often be found working with her to complete tasks that could be managed by children. The youngest refugees flocked to her to hear stories and legends from Naboo. She would entertain them for hours, freeing up the adults to work on recovery and relocation efforts. Their parents watched indulgently, glad to see their younglings happy, but all the while, fear tightened around them.

The sun had something they needed to live. They could not simply be relocated. They needed to find a specific environment, and time was against them. The girl didn't understand, not entirely. To her, light was light. It wasn't until the adults began to get sick that the severity of the situation became real to her. It wasn't until the children followed that she began to panic. Through her fear she nursed them, giving comfort where she could and never betraying her terror as the sickness grew worse.

They all died. Thousands of them. Every single one. Without their sun, they could not survive. No scientist could replicate what they needed; no new world could be found for them. Without safe harbor, they went extinct. The galaxy was a poorer place without them.

The girl mourned. Her father wasn't sure what to say to her. That sometimes this happened. Sometimes the mission failed. He let her cry and rage and grieve. And when the initial storm of that had passed, they made their way home together. She spent a lot of time in the garden by herself, watering flowers, surrounding herself with growing things and new life. Her father understood. It was important to remember, after a tragedy like the one she'd witnessed, that life persisted, even if its form was different.

They didn't talk about it very much, the girl and her father. Not when the girl decided to go into politics. Not when she was elected queen. Not even when she left Naboo to serve in the Galactic Senate. But the tragedy always loomed at the back of her decision-making. No matter how well she planned or how well prepared she was, she knew that she could fail. She knew the cost could be too high to fully comprehend. She had already learned that sometimes the full weight of the galaxy was stacked against her.

Padmé Naberrie got out of bed every single morning and tried again.

CHAPTER 24

Padmé felt it was necessary to explain herself to the Wookiees. If nothing else, they deserved to know that their droid had been compromised. She genuinely liked the captains and wanted them to know that they had helped her. She made her way to the flight deck and found G-1FY already there, waiting for her. He was twisting his metal fingers awkwardly and looking as apologetic as a protocol droid could.

"I am ready, Senator," the droid said. "I hope they will not be too angry with me."

"It wasn't your fault, Iffy," Padmé reminded him.

She led the way to where the Wookiees sat, flying the ship in tandem fine-tuned by years of practice. Without the accoutrement of G-1FY's dinner, the flight deck was a little bit less welcoming to observers, but very much more interesting. The Wookiees reached easily for control panels that Padmé would have had to stretch to her limits to access. Brown-furred limbs moved smoothly as the ship streaked through space, never colliding or interfering with each other. Pilot and navigator, they were a perfect team, each relying on the other's talents for a safe arrival and never doubting their skill.

"Captains? Do you have a moment?" Padmé asked. Flying through hyperspace didn't require constant attention once the course was set, but Rayyne tended to stay on top of her systems at all times, much like Idda was rarely parted from the engines.

The two Wookiees turned to look at her, and Naijoh trilled an affirmative.

"My name is Padmé, which you already know, but you might know me better as Amidala," she said. "I am a senator for the Galactic Republic from the planet Naboo. Your employer wanted me to see your operation and arranged for me to learn that your trade network existed. We decided to take a closer look and join a ship on a resupply mission to the Outer Rim. We—Captain Typho and I—chose your ship because, well, because you seemed like you were the best."

Rayyne clapped her husband on the back of his furry head and made the sound Padmé could identify as Wookiee laughter. Padmé was relieved that neither of them seemed angry with her. She did not want to deal with angry Wookiees if she could possibly avoid it.

"She said she told him you were up to something," G-1FY supplied. "And now he owes her—"

A trill from Rayyne made him stop translating. It wasn't possible for a droid to blush, but G-1FY managed to convey the emotion anyway.

"I was going to say 'a brush,'" G-1FY said primly. Rayyne laughed again.

"I'm sorry for the deception," Padmé said. "Before we left, I wanted you to know the truth. You have done a great service to the Republic, and also to me. Thank you."

"The only thing I am upset about is having to replace you," Naijoh said, speaking through the droid. "Both you and Captain Typho were excellent security personnel. If you ever want to come back, just let us know. Idda is going to miss you."

Padmé thanked them again and left G-1FY to explain his programming glitch on his own. She hoped he could be fixed without too much trouble. They were already talking about diagnostics before she was out of hearing range. He would be all right.

When she returned to her quarters, it occurred to her that since everyone on the *Namrelllew* knew who she was, she could access her private communications. She'd been away from Coruscant for long enough that the messages would be piling up, even with Sabé triaging them for her. She couldn't deal with anything that required advanced security, of course, but she could take the opportunity to get ahead of her low-priority correspondence.

She dug her datapad out of her pack, where it was hidden under the false bottom. The first message she noticed when she turned it on was from Bail. She'd have to deal with that later. There was one from Saché that was marked low-security, and she opened it enthusiastically. It had been too long since she had talked with her friends. She sat cross-legged on her berth and leaned against the wall, making herself comfortable.

Saché's message was predominately about Karlini tea, confirming what Padmé had guessed when she talked to Oje N'deeb. There was a sentence at the end indicating that Saché wanted a return call, and after a quick check of the time, Padmé established the connection. In a matter of minutes, a figure of Saché was balanced on her hand.

"Padmé! I'm so glad to hear from you," Saché said. "Everything is well?"

"Yes," Padmé said. "I think you and I have been working on the same project from different ends."

"Give me a moment," Saché said. "I've got some company."

She stepped out of the projector's range, and Padmé could hear her issuing orders to some of the children. There was laughter in the background. Padmé's heart ached. A true family home was years away for her, but she knew that Anakin wanted it, too.

"All right," Saché said, reappearing. "I've banished all the little ears to the garden. What have you been up to?"

"I ended up on a ship delivering Karlini tea," Padmé said. "I was curious, because we're quite far out from the Core. Eventually, I talked to someone in, shall we say, management, and they admitted to buying the tea in an attempt to get on my good side."

"Your good side?" Saché said. "Do you have a stake on Karlinus that I don't know about?"

"I think he meant more generally," Padmé said. "Anyway, when I saw your message, I thought I would tell you that I have begun investigating the buyer, but they seem to check out."

"I still don't understand why anyone would think Karlini tea impresses you," Saché said.

"He's Neimoidian," Padmé said. Saché's hand went to her face, to the scars that traced her skin. "It's a splinter group, if you can imagine. They want to rehabilitate the image of the entire Trade Federation."

"That would take some doing," Saché said. Her voice was neutral. "And you're . . . okay with this?"

"It's too good an opportunity to pass up, politically at least," Padmé said. "As for my personal feelings . . . I don't expect you to share them, but maybe it's time I moved on? I've never been comfortable with how the Neimoidians make me feel. And now, for the first time, when I think of them the first feeling that comes to me isn't hate."

Saché was quiet for a moment. It was hard for both of them to admit their flaws, and Saché wasn't quite ready to move past her anger just yet.

"I'll back you, of course," Saché said after taking a moment to think. "Just . . . don't invite me to any of the parties."

"Understood," Padmé said. She tapped her fingers on the mattress she was sitting on. "What I can't figure out is how Governor Kelma is dealing with the increase in labor demands."

"Oh," said Saché. She stilled as everything clicked into place. "I know. I think your Neimoidian friend has been freeing enslaved people and funneling them to Karlinus. There's been a significant uptick in immigration. Kelma doesn't dig too deeply, because that's how the system works, but she took me and Harli Jafan out to meet with a few of her new citizens unofficially, and they were all from systems in the Outer Rim where the Separatists have made incursions."

"He didn't mention that part," Padmé said. "I wonder why."

"Maybe you should ask him," Saché said. It didn't sound as painful as it might have. "He's making profit on the tea and the rest of whatever he's selling, but the only thing he's gaining from mass emancipation is your attention."

"And the rehabilitation of the Trade Federation," Padmé mused.

"That's going to take more than a few hundred people," Saché said. Her voice darkened.

"Yes," Padmé agreed, "but it's a start."

They talked about the children for a while after that. The original group of adoptees from the Occupation were mostly away at school for the semester. Saché was very proud of them. Yané's new additions to the family, the mudslide survivors, were settling in. They still had nightmares, and a few of them were aggressively claustrophobic, but they were all making good progress toward healing.

"And congratulations," Saché said cautiously. "About the other thing. With the dress."

Padmé couldn't help the wide smile that dawned on her face. She would never be able to share the news publicly, but hearing from those closest to her brought her a warm glow. She'd tell Sabé as soon as she got home. Sabé deserved to hear it in person, not put together the clues or hear it over the holonet.

"Thank you," she said. "Yané did incredible work."

"And you're happy?" Saché asked.

"Yes," Padmé said. Another wide smile graced her face. "Yes, I am."

They talked about a few other inconsequential matters for a moment before a disturbance on Saché's end drew their conversation to a close. One of the kids had fallen in the pond, and the ensuing commotion was enough to end the call. Saché was laughing when she signed off, though, and Padmé was glad to see that she was so happy. Before her good mood could temper itself with cynicism, Padmé turned her comm back on and sent a call to Oje N'deeb.

"Senator Amidala," he said, appearing in her palm. Too late, she wished she'd stood up to make the call. "I take it you have made a decision?"

"You didn't tell me about the people you were sending to Karlinus," Padmé said by way of greeting.

"No," N'deeb said.

"Why not?" Padmé asked.

"You would have had no reason to believe me," N'deeb said. "And I thought it might appear self-aggrandizing."

"You said that someone else had the idea to buy the tea," Padmé said. "Was it your idea to help enslaved people?"

"It was," N'deeb admitted. "Your voting record is public, after all. There have been several failed bills about trying to expand Republic antislavery laws into the Outer Rim without expanding the actual Republic. You've voted in favor of every single one of them and spoken about them in the Senate. I knew that it was a cause that meant something to you. More than tea."

"Much more than tea," Padmé said. "Are you using Trade Federation money?"

"Much as I'd like to, no," he said. "The credits are mine. My family's legacy is, as you can imagine, more than a little bit checkered. It seemed like the least I could do."

"It's more than most would do," Padmé said.

"It's exactly what you would do," N'deeb said. He looked

at her with almost unnerving directness, considering he was a hologram.

"I'll bring your cause to Senator Organa and the rest of my faction," Padmé said. "I can't imagine any circumstances under which he would turn you down. He doesn't have my history with the Trade Federation, and he's much, much more patient than I am. But it won't be easy. There will be considerable opposition from regular senators and from the Trade Federation cronies. When your representative comes to Coruscant, and I sincerely hope they do, they will have an ally in me."

"Thank you, Senator," N'deeb said. He blinked his wide black eyes slowly as he inclined his head to her. "I look forward to working with you."

The hologram in her hand disappeared as the call disconnected, and Padmé leaned her head back against the cool metal of the hull. The plating vibrated slightly from the power of the engines, hurtling the *Namrelllew* through hyperspace, but even that was comforting. Her mission had been wildly successful. The Republic had gained a powerful ally. It might gain a whole new system. Captains Naijoh and Rayyne could be trusted for any future transportation requirements in the Outer Rim. Oje N'deeb's entire network was at her disposal. And every new citizen on Karlinus was a direct slap in the face of traffickers.

But she couldn't get the siege on Hebekrr Minor out of her head. It wasn't exactly the way Saché and Yané had described the camps, but the feeling of being trapped had to be a little bit similar. How many people across the galaxy were stuck like that right now? How many were under fire? How many were hungry? How many were scared? And how hollow must her victories sound when told to a parent who couldn't take care of their child or to a child whose parent was never coming home again?

She wouldn't solve all the problems in the galaxy. She couldn't. But she wasn't about to let that stop her. It never had before. Padmé got off her bed and started packing up her quarters. She was going home, but her work was far from done.

CHAPTER 25

It was almost over. Padmé and Typho were on their return journey, and soon Sabé would be able to put aside Amidala and go back to being just herself again. Although she had made up her mind about what she wanted to do next, she felt antsy. Uncomfortable. She couldn't quite shake the feeling that she was being selfish or cowardly, and she didn't know if that little voice was telling her the truth or if it was just being a jerk.

"You need to eat something fried," Mariek said as Sabé fidgeted her way around the sitting room. She couldn't get comfortable. "Something that protocol droid would disapprove of."

"Are you offering an escape plan?" Sabé asked. "Because as much as I like the idea, I don't think I can focus enough to plot."

"There's a first time for everything," Mariek said. "Go get changed and I'll take care of everything else."

"Thanks, Mariek," Sabé said. The guard captain nodded.

Sabé picked out one of her Tatooine outfits. It was rugged and the colors were dull. She would fit in in the seedier parts of Coruscant without turning any heads. She put on makeup, using contouring to ensure that she didn't look like Amidala or even herself. By the time she was dressed, she knew exactly where she wanted to go. Mariek didn't say anything when Sabé told her where they were headed, just passed over an extra vibroblade and ran a check of the emergency comm.

Dex's hadn't changed.

Sabé slid across the hard duraplast bench to wedge herself into the corner of the diner. From here, she could see the entryway and the kitchen. She knew there were at least three other exits, not counting the windows, but this was safe enough for now. She rested her fingers on the table and waited for the server droid to come take her order.

As she sat and listened, Sabé realized that though Dex's was physically the same as when she and Tonra used to come here, something *had* changed about the menu. Fully half of it was blocked off. When she asked the droid about it, she was told that some ingredients were unavailable and that Dex was looking into new supply chains now that the war was on.

"It's a menace, this war," Dex said from behind the counter. The Besalisk had lumbered out of the kitchen while Sabé was talking to the droid. "So many things we can't get or are suddenly more expensive. The folk down here are going to notice the pinch long before those in the upper levels consider doing anything about it."

"But they will eventually, right?" Sabé asked.

"Oh, they'll try," Dex said. "They'll write a bill and talk

about it for a week, and maybe it'll pass or it won't, but I'll still be here, trying to run a restaurant."

He would never say it out loud, but there was no doubt in Sabé's mind that Dex would turn to the black market long before then. A lot of bad people were about to make a lot of credits.

"One crate in the right place can change everything," Dex said. "Those up there don't think about things that small."

He reached over his shoulder with one of his four arms, then set the stew Sabé had always ordered when she came here in front of her. She smiled. She should have known she couldn't fool him for long.

"Thanks, Dex," she said.

He went back to work as she ate, but she thought about what he'd said. One crate. The right place. Padmé was going to make differences from Coruscant, and they would be big ones. Sabé was choosing another path, but her narrower scope didn't make her less helpful or relevant. She might save fewer people than Padmé did, but she would know their faces.

When Mariek signaled that it was time to go, Sabé had a full stomach and a quiet mind. She was ready.

It was late in the evening on Coruscant when the *Namrelllew* finally received its landing permit. Padmé and Typho said their farewells briefly—well, as briefly as one could when a Mriss had attached herself to one's knees and refused to let go—and then hired a private shuttle to the Senate building. Senator Organa was waiting for her report and she wanted to make it in person at his office.

Padmé's office was empty when she arrived. She had half hoped that Sabé and the others would still be there, because she wanted to see them. However, duty called, and their reunion would have to be delayed a bit longer while Padmé tied up the loose ends.

They kept an emergency change of clothes in one of the compartments at the back of her office. Padmé couldn't remember what dress they had stashed away at the moment but was pleasantly surprised to find a dark green gown that fastened at the front. She retrieved the matching shoes and headpiece from the bottom of the compartment and then turned to excuse herself to the refresher.

"Do you need any help?" Typho asked. To his credit, he looked only slightly terrified.

"No." Padmé stifled a giggle. "This one is designed for me to put it on without help."

It took her about five minutes to peel off her pilot uniform and dispose of the soft linen undergarments she wore beneath it. Changing into fresh clothes would have been nicer with access to her bathtub first, but she was in a hurry. She pulled on the new clothes, starting with light trousers and an undershirt. The dress was heavy green velvet lined with golden Karlini silk. The silk was sewn right in, instead of being a separate underdress, which made the outfit easier to manage on her own. She fastened the metallic gold buttons, stepped into her dull gold shoes, and clipped on the decorative armbands that covered her from wrist to elbow.

Once unbraided, her hair fell in soft waves that almost looked like she'd done them on purpose. The headpiece was a simple band of beaten gold that would keep her hair out of her face. Dormé would have pinned the bulk of her hair into a net to complete the look, but Padmé was on a tight schedule. She surveyed herself in the mirror when she was done, making sure everything was in place. There was no denying it: Senator Amidala was back.

In her office, Typho had managed to find an extra uniform jacket and had changed into it. He needed a shave, but that would have to wait.

"I'm ready, Captain," Senator Amidala said. "Let's go talk to Bail."

At this time of the day, the halls of the Senate were mostly empty. With the chamber released from debate, everyone was either working in their offices or already engaged for the evening. There were cleaning droids to avoid and the odd messenger droid that beeped judgmentally if impeded, but Padmé made it to Bail's office without being intercepted by anyone who wanted to talk.

She knocked on the door, and it slid open immediately. She nodded to Typho, who would stay in the hallway, and walked into the room. Bail was standing by the window, his muted blue cape dark against the night behind him. Mon Mothma was seated by the desk, immaculate as usual in her customary white gown. To Padmé's surprise, Chancellor Palpatine had joined them. He stood by Bail and smiled widely when she came into the room.

"Senator Amidala, it is wonderful to see you returned," the Chancellor said. Padmé knew he hadn't been informed of the mission before she left and wondered when Bail had decided to tell him.

"Thank you, Chancellor," Padmé said. "It's good to be back."

"I was quite surprised when I spoke with you a few nights ago, only to realize you were somewhere else," the Chancellor said. "Senator Organa was kind enough to explain. I assume your trip was a success?"

Padmé had been planning to give her report to Bail, which was more of a conversation between friends than anything else, especially this late in the day. She was exhausted, but she'd never let that stop her before. She drew herself up to give a formal account.

"I went to Hebekrr Minor to investigate some information given to us by the Jedi," Padmé said. "A contact wished to meet with a senator, specifically me, it turns out."

"Why you?" asked Mon Mothma.

"He's Neimoidian," Padmé said. "He knew he'd get my attention."

"Neimoidian?" said Bail. "What could a Neimoidian possibly expect to get from you?"

"He wants Lott Dod's Trade Federation Senate seat," Padmé said. "And I think we should help him get it."

Everyone in the room was a professional politician, so it was a few seconds before anyone reacted.

"You would help him gain power?" Palpatine said. The Chancellor maintained his usual calm presence, but a strange and quiet anger simmered under his voice. "After what we suffered during the Occupation?"

"I didn't like the idea at first," Padmé admitted. "Even though the political benefits are obvious. But he—and his company—have been actively trying to repair damage in the Outer Rim. They're not price gouging, they're not selling arms. And, most important, they are actively seeking out enslaved people to free and sending them to Karlinus so they can get back on their feet."

"This is too good to pass up," Bail said. "Even with the Trade Federation's history, a chance of destabilizing them like this? We couldn't ask for a better opportunity."

"I agree," Mon Mothma said. "And I appreciate that this is difficult for you. I will help you in any way I can."

"This is something to consider," Palpatine said slowly.

He blinked several times, and a look of calculated control flashed across his face. "But I'm afraid I must excuse myself. The Chancellor isn't supposed to get involved with Senate appointments."

Neither, technically speaking, were senators, but it was a rare politician who showed up on Coruscant with no allies at all.

The Chancellor made his exit, and Padmé finally sat down in the chair next to Mon Mothma's. She was tired, but she could last a little while longer. Bail sat down behind his desk and folded his hands on the polished surface.

"Sabé did an incredible job," he said. "I'm still not sure how the Chancellor figured it out. He came to me after a party I hosted, concerned for your safety since a double had been present. I didn't tell him everything."

"Thank you," Padmé said.

"Were you able to observe any fighting on the front?" Mon Mothma asked. "We've only had accounts from the Jedi."

"The situation on Hebekrr Minor was worse than we were expecting," Padmé said. She allowed herself to slump in the chair. "The main city was under siege. The clone troopers had bolstered fortifications, and the Jedi were overseeing the defense. It was a small incursion, only a few thousand droids."

"So everything worked like it was supposed to?" Bail said. "In terms of cooperation, at least?"

"As far as I could tell, yes," Padmé said. "Commander

Sticks—that's what the clone in charge calls himself—was treated with respect by everyone, and so were all of his men."

"Yet you said it was worse?" Mon Mothma said.

"The Separatists wanted the magistrate to sign a treaty," Padmé said. It was a familiar story. "She wouldn't, and they couldn't get at her to threaten her directly. Instead, they traveled hundreds of kilometers to kidnap her family. That was right before we arrived. When they realized that our shuttle wouldn't be immediately associated with the Republic, they requested our help."

"And you gave it," Bail said.

"I worked with Commander Sticks on a plan, and we flew them to the Separatist camp," Padmé said. "We had to defend the landing bay, and the extraction was a bit hotter than anyone expected, but there were no casualties on our side."

"Senators should not be directly engaged in this fighting," Mon Mothma said.

"With all respect, Senator," Padmé said, "that is exactly why you sent someone like me on this mission. You don't approve of violence, and you never will. I admire that, and I have accepted it. All I ask in return is that you accept that I am the person you send when there's the possibility of . . . aggressive negotiations."

It was the closest they'd ever come to having it out. Mon Mothma considered Padmé's words for a moment and then nodded.

"As you say, Senator Amidala," she said.

"Anything else?" Bail asked, clearly hoping that there wasn't.

"Hebekrr is going to petition for admission to the Republic," Padmé said. "I don't know if they'll go through with it, but they need the protection of our army."

Bail rubbed his forehead.

"We all know that's not how the Republic is supposed to expand," he said. "I don't like the idea of us running some sort of racket like a common cartel, but I think it's something that's going to come up in the future. And it's better that they join us than join the Separatists."

"Those were my thoughts, as well," Padmé said.

Bail looked tired, and even Mon Mothma was starting to droop a little bit at the shoulders. Padmé knew they were both working endlessly to secure the future of the Republic, and she was glad that she had returned to help them do it. In spite of herself, she yawned.

"Apologies," she said. "I am hyper-lagged."

"Of course," Bail said. "We'll see you tomorrow?"

"Bright and early," Padmé said. She yawned again. "Maybe not too early."

"Good night, senators." Mon Mothma rose gracefully, and they all went their separate ways.

The calming dark of Chancellor Palpatine's office was broken by the white-hot rage of Darth Sidious. It burned through him like a cleansing fire, rooting out his doubts and his troubles, distilling his emotions to the absolute conviction that made him so strong. Lightning arced from the tips of his fingers to ground itself in the dark sculpture he kept in his office for occasions such as this, when all he wanted was to destroy.

How *dare* they? After all the time he had spent manipulating the Trade Federation, bending it to his will. After his investments and guidance and threats. How dare some upstart develop a conscience and decide to try fixing what he had so carefully broken?

It would be easy enough to snuff the traitor out. To nip this petty rebellion in the bud and turn everyone's attention back to the legacy he wanted the Trade Federation to preserve.

But Sidious hesitated. He had not come so far in life by acting rashly and without significant forethought. This rogue Neimoidian was strengthening the Outer Rim, bolstering the people there with supplies and morale and the knowledge that some systems in the galaxy still worked. That could be turned to his purpose. It would draw the war out. It would give the Outer Rim a chance. It would make them all the more bitter with the Republic when that chance was crushed. No, he would not kill the traitor yet. He would let him do his work, find his redemption. It would make his eventual destruction all the sweeter.

Sidious pressed his hands against the black stone and felt his stored hate and anger seething back at him. This was his endurance. This was why he would win. He knew the channels of power in the galaxy, and he knew how to shift them and work them to his advantage.

"Tyranus," he said, and the comm connected him to his apprentice.

"Master?" He could never seem to catch Dooku off guard, no matter what hour he called. "Did you require something of me?"

"There has been a development on Hebekrr Minor," Sidious said. "The Trade Federation is to stay out of it."

"There have been rumors of a splinter group within the Trade Federation, Master," Dooku said. "Gunray and the others already seek action in response."

"Then hold them back," Sidious ordered. "I wish this to develop before it is crushed."

"As you say, Master," Dooku said, and disappeared.

Having an apprentice who actually enjoyed dealing with Separatist politics—not to mention threatening Separatist politicians—was one of the best ideas Sidious had had lately. Nute Gunray drove him to distraction.

With the matter delegated appropriately, Darth Sidious turned his thoughts back to his favorite subject: the domination of the galaxy, and billions suffering at his command.

CHAPTER 26

The easiest way to get Padmé alone was to be the handmaiden who helped her get ready for bed, and so, for one last time, Sabé put on the hooded orange robe and pulled the cowl up over her hair. This was the outfit Rabé and Eirtaé had designed to draw attention. This was the silk Yané had shredded to send the messages Saché had carried through the camp. The bright color swallowed them up, made them icons instead of people. There were windowpanes in Theed that were decorated with this image, and no thought given to the girl inside.

It was her first suit of armor, and Sabé needed it.

She waited in Padmé's room for her friend to return. She knew that Padmé would go to the Senate first. She'd left early so they wouldn't run into each other, exiting discreetly so anyone who saw Amidala later on would assume she'd never left. To the end, she played the role she had chosen all those years ago, when Captain Panaka had come to interview her. Her heart would let her do no less, even if it was breaking.

She heard in the lower level the noise of Padmé arriving home. C-3PO greeted her, his voice carrying through the apartment as he bustled around asking if he should find her something to eat. Sabé heard the quiet murmur of Padmé's voice, presumably saying no and then bidding Captain Typho good night. Sabé could have gone out into the antechamber. They could have sat comfortably and talked. No one would have disturbed them. But Sabé wanted this to happen in the room where Padmé was most likely to be herself.

"Leave the cases, Threepio." Padmé's voice was much closer now. "We'll see to them in the morning."

"Good night, Senator," C-3PO said. "And, if I may say so, it is nice to have you back with us."

Padmé thanked him and then walked into her bedroom.

"Oh," she said when she saw Sabé sitting at the foot of the bed. The stress of her job—covert and otherwise—fell away at once. "I am so glad to see you."

"I'm glad you're home safely," Sabé said. "Come and let me comb your hair before it ties itself into permanent knots."

Padmé smiled—her true smile, not the senatorial one—and went to sit at her dressing table. Sabé stood behind her with the comb, removed the golden band, and began to deal with her hair.

"Your husband says hello," Sabé said after a few moments of silence.

All of Padmé's defences slammed back into place. Sabé knew it was a habit—necessary for survival, even—but watching from the outside was not something she liked at all. The hurt it caused was almost immeasurable.

"Sabé, I—" Padmé began, but Sabé held up her free hand, the other still moving through Padmé's hair.

"We didn't exactly have a lot of time before you left," Sabé said. "And we always put work first. But it still hurt, to find out from him."

"I was selfish," Padmé said. For someone so tiny, she rarely seemed small. Now it was like she was folding in on herself. "Having you back with me was so wonderful. Even though things were different, I didn't want anything to change. I was wrong, and I am sorry."

"Thank you," Sabé said. Her heart cracked in her chest. "I liked things being the way they were, too. But I don't think we can do that anymore."

Padmé was silent for a moment. It felt like an eternity.

"With the war, there's going to be a lot of new challenges," Padmé said. Parts of the senator emerged as she spoke. The parts Sabé hadn't been able to replicate. The parts Padmé had built without her. "I don't know what's coming, but I'm glad you'll be here with me."

Sabé froze, the comb stopping mid-stroke. She'd have to be clearer, even if it broke them both. Padmé looked up and met her eyes in the mirror.

"I won't be here," Sabé said. "Please don't ask me."

For the first time since they were fourteen years old, the distance between them was incalculable.

"What?" said Padmé. "Why? I don't understand."

Sabé put the comb down on the dressing table and retreated to sit on the end of the bed again. Padmé turned around but didn't stand up to follow her. She understood that Sabé needed space.

"When you were gone? I tried," Sabé said. It all came rushing out of her: the feelings and emotions she'd tamped down since her arrival on Coruscant. "I tried so hard to be Amidala the way we used to. But I couldn't. She's changed. You've changed. And Anakin is only a part of it."

"How have I changed?" Padmé asked. She seemed desperate to know. "Is it the war?"

"It's not just the war," Sabé said. Suddenly she was so tired she thought her bones were made of lead. "It's all the politics. The talking and the parties and the dealmaking and the backchat. I know that the Senate needs all that to operate, and you're really good at it. And I could be really good at it. I was you and almost no one noticed. But I can't. I've changed, too. I can't fight this war your way."

Padmé leaned forward to rest her hands on her knees. It occurred to Sabé that she was probably exhausted, too. But this conversation wouldn't wait, especially now that they'd started it. They had to have it all out, now.

"When I got here it was hard," Padmé said. "Thinking about people as concepts. Reducing huge numbers to line items in a document. All of that sort of thing."

"I remember," Sabé said.

"If it's easier now, is that bad?" Padmé asked. It wasn't the senator asking.

Sabé considered her answer.

"For some people, yes," Sabé said. "The Jedi, for example. They don't even get upset when their friends die. It's all about balance and the eternal Force. That's why they're so bad at politics. They value all life, and they lack practicality. But I think you'll be all right. At the end of the day, even the longest and hardest ones, you'll remember."

Padmé stood up and came to sit beside her. She pressed Sabé's hand between hers and leaned her head on Sabé's shoulder. Sabé never wanted to let her go, even as she prepared to leave her.

"How will you remember?" Padmé asked. "How will you fight?"

"I'll go back to Tatooine for now," Sabé said. "We're starting to see results. It's small-scale compared to what you do, I know, but it makes more sense to me. It makes me feel like I'm doing something."

"I understand," Padmé said. "This mission, while we were on Hebekrr Minor, we rescued a family being held hostage. It wasn't the most important part for the Senate, but it kind of was for me."

Sabé rested her cheek on the top of Padmé's head. She would miss her so much. For ten years, Padmé had been the center of her galaxy, the lodestar by which she made all of her decisions. She'd never imagined outgrowing that. But life had other ideas.

"Do you like Anakin?" Padmé asked. She sounded like the girl she'd been, huddled under blankets, asking questions about Harli Jafan all those years ago. "You're really the only one who has spent any time with him as an adult."

"I understand why *you* like Anakin," Sabé said. "He's a little bit intense for me. He's completely devoted to you, which I admire, but when he's angry, he scares me a little bit."

"He's very powerful in a way I could never understand," Padmé said. "His sense of justice is extreme. There was an incident with a Tusken encampment on Tatooine when we were there."

"That was Anakin?" Sabé said. "They're talking about that massacre on the other side of the planet."

"It was awful," Padmé said. "I tried to talk to him about it afterward, but I didn't get very far. And then we got the message from Obi-Wan, and then Geonosis happened, and then—"

"And then you got married," Sabé said. She tried not to sound judgmental, but it was a challenge.

Padmé turned her head to bury her face in Sabé's shoulder.

"When you say it like that, it sounds terrible," she said, voice muffled by the fabric. "But at the time, I couldn't imagine doing anything else. I still can't."

"You told me once that when you gave your heart to

someone, it would be a disaster," Sabé reminded her. "I should have known you weren't exaggerating."

"It's just always so thrilling," Padmé said. There was something in her voice that spoke of dreams Sabé had never had, but could understand wanting. "We never stop to work anything out because we're always stealing a moment alone together or crashing into the next mission."

"It sounds romantic," Sabé said drily.

"It sounds like a holonovel," Padmé admitted. "The only time we've had to ourselves—to *be* ourselves—was at the lake house, and even then, I was in hiding. But we had time. And we talked. We talked so much. I want that again."

"Well, Anakin seems hell-bent on slicing every Separatist in half, and I wouldn't want to get in your way on the Senate floor," Sabé said. "Between the two of you, you'll probably end the war as quickly as possible. You'll still have to be clandestine after that, of course, but at least you'll be able to talk."

Padmé sat up and looked right at her.

"Are you making fun of me?" she demanded.

"Yes," Sabé said. "But I also think I'm right."

"Thank you." Padmé sighed. "All this time, all the things I've asked you to do or give up or put on hold. I'm sorry that I pushed you further than you wanted to go this time. I couldn't have made it this far without you."

Sabé turned, taking both of Padmé's hands in hers. Their lives had been linked in a way that was hard to explain, their identities entwined for the good of Naboo. And now that was over. They would have separate paths. Sabé would learn to cast her own shadow. She faced her queen, her senator, her friend, and gave her a sad smile.

"My hands are yours," she said. "Please don't ask me for them again."

Padmé nodded, tears in her eyes, because she couldn't speak.

$$\text{꜀꜀꜀꜀}$$

They dressed themselves for bed and climbed beneath the covers. An invitation had been neither extended nor accepted, but the understanding between them had not changed. There were many things they had never needed to talk about, and both of them felt like they'd had enough serious conversation for the evening.

Instead they pulled the blanket over their heads and giggled long into the night, like they had done when they were girls. They remembered the concert and the other ways they had tormented Quarsh Panaka. They talked about that election day at the lake house, when Tonra had looked at Sabé and Sabé had finally allowed herself to look back. They talked about the others, too. Rabé's career and Eirtaé's work. Yané and Saché's ever-increasing number of children. They mourned Cordé and Versé, and each of them reminded the other how lucky they were to have Dormé.

Sabé fell asleep first, and Padmé looked at her face in the dim light. It had always been said that they were nearly identical. Padmé knew that wasn't true, but she had spent almost half her life taking advantage of the illusion. Tonight, for the first time, she saw the lines on Sabé's face that she didn't share. The wear of the desert sun, the worry of a hundred cargo runs when the cargo was living, breathing souls.

Sabé had always had a separate life. Padmé had always done what she could to make sure her friend was happy. And if this was what it took, then this was what she would do. Sabé deserved to leave Padmé's shadow, if she wanted to. The others had, in their own ways, and now it was Sabé's turn. This hurt the most, but Padmé would never tell her. Sabé had dedicated years of her life to Amidala, the same years that Padmé herself had given.

And now it was time to let her go.

CHAPTER 27

It wasn't much like coming home, but it was close enough. As Tatooine grew larger in the shuttle window, Sabé couldn't regret any of the decisions that had brought her here. She'd been away from Coruscant for only a short while—the time it took for Mariek to take her to the transport hub—and then to catch a shuttle, and already she felt calmer, more sure of herself. The part of her that was Amidala was sad to give up the lights and power in the Galactic Core, but the part of her that was Sabé knew she had made the right choice.

Tonra met her in the shuttle bay. He smiled when he caught sight of her in the crowd, and as soon as she got within arm's reach, he swept her up into a hug. She wondered if this was what Padmé felt when she saw Anakin after they'd been separated. Then she decided she didn't care.

"I'm so glad you're back," Tonra said.

"I know you didn't miss my cooking," Sabé said. He laughed.

"No, I did not," he said. "But we started this together. It's better when you're here."

She took his hand—posing as a married couple had its

advantages—and they set off for their house. Mos Eisley hadn't changed. The streets were still packed with merchants hawking questionable goods, and people trying to make it from one day to the next. The suns were hot. The wind didn't help anything at all. And Sabé already had sand in her teeth.

When they reached the house, Sabé unpacked quickly while Tonra brewed some caf and set out the hard biscuits he'd made the day before. Sabé sat across from him and took a bite of one.

"Do you want to talk about it?" Tonra asked after taking a sip of his caf.

For a moment, Sabé wasn't sure. But then she decided that not only did she want to talk about it, she wanted to talk about it with him, specifically. Of everyone who had ever worked with Padmé Amidala, he might understand the best.

"I think I quit," Sabé said. "I told her to never ask me to come back."

Tonra peeled her fingers off her mug and squeezed them.

The story spilled out of her then. All the wretchedness of Senate politics on Coruscant. The way she'd felt more out of place and wrong every time she put on one of Amidala's dresses. How awful it was to finally confront Padmé and sort everything out with her. It was like she couldn't stop talking. And for once she didn't have to, though she did leave Anakin's part in the story out of it. She respected Padmé's privacy in that regard. Tonra didn't interrupt her, and he never let go of her hand.

"Do you want a hug?" he asked when she was finally done.

"Yes," she whispered. She felt drained and empty, new and sure.

Tonra stood up and drew her into his arms. This was different than the hug at the docking bay. That had been happiness and comradery. This was the promise of a solid foundation, wherever she decided to stand.

"I always knew she wouldn't pick me," she said into his chest. He stroked her hair. "I just thought that she would pick *more*. Like a planet. Or a species."

He held her tightly for a while longer, and then he stepped back. When she looked up, she saw the fondness in his face that used to scare her so much.

"Do you want to see what you picked?" he asked.

"Yes?" she said, ready to agree with him even if she didn't know what he was talking about.

He laughed and went to the table they used as a desk. He opened a drawer and drew out a box.

"Open it," he said, passing it over.

Sabé keyed the latch open and flipped the lid. Inside the box was a small device unlike anything she had ever seen before. It seemed to be assembled from random parts. As she looked closer, she realized it was a scanner of some kind.

"This is how they find the chips," she said. She held freedom in her hands, and she had never felt more powerful.

"With some modifications, yes," Tonra said. "Our contact gave me one when I told them we might be able to improve it."

"And by 'we' you mean Rabé?" Sabé asked.

"Yes," Tonra said. "The device itself has to be low-tech, because it has to be easy to replicate with whatever parts are available. Ideally, they'd like them to work on other planets, but right now they're just focused on Tatooine. The problem was the programming. The chips would cycle, and they'd have to start from scratch."

"High-end programming in an innocuous-looking device is right up Rabé's alley," Sabé said.

"I noticed," Tonra said. "She also sent several modifications that we could try, and a high-tech version, should that ever be useful."

"And it works?" Sabé asked.

"To quote my contact, it works, and it keeps working," Tonra said. "It cycles faster than the chips do, and always stays ahead of their counterprogramming. The organization here is looking forward to some expansion."

"Including us?" Sabé asked. "I think the water plant has probably fired me by now."

"I didn't want to answer for you while you were gone," Tonra said. "But yes, it includes us."

She set the box down and hugged him a third time. She

could feel his surprise even as his arms wrapped around her again. She didn't usually show this much affection, even when they were on-again. She looked up at him and smiled.

"I need some time, I think," she said. "To figure out who I am, when I don't have to be her."

"I understand," he said. "You have all the time you need from me, you know that."

"I do," Sabé said. "But I was wondering if maybe you would like to help?"

Kissing him *was* like coming home. It struck her, because it never had been before. There had always been Amidala in the back of her mind, but now the shadow was gone, and she had Tatooine's two stars to light her way. She smiled against his mouth, and he laughed. She wanted to stay in the moment forever, but she also knew there would be more in the future if she moved forward.

"Shall I introduce you to the White Suns?" he asked.

"Yes," said Sabé.

She was ready to get to work.

CHAPTER 28

Their schedules rarely overlapped, but Padmé kept her evenings free. They arranged for secure communications via the droids that served them so faithfully. Now that Anakin was a Jedi Knight, he could come and go from the Temple more freely. Perhaps Obi-Wan wondered where he went, but he would never ask. Anakin's time on Coruscant was his own, for the most part, and the time he didn't spend with Chancellor Palpatine he jealously guarded for Padmé.

Her apartment would be dark when he reached it. Her handmaidens left her alone at night now. He knew that some of them at least suspected the truth, and he appreciated their discretion. The guards, he avoided.

C-3PO was invariably there to meet him and take his cloak. Sometimes Anakin had R2-D2 with him, and the two droids would talk, but more often C-3PO would wander off and make himself scarce after saying hello. At first it was hard for Anakin to see the droid. There were so many memories in those wires, each scrap of metal and line of programming eked out of next to nothing while he was enslaved under the Tatooine suns. C-3PO was the last thing in the galaxy that he had shared with his mother. Giving him to Padmé was the only gift he could really manage. As a Jedi, he had nothing else to give.

But as he had told her all those years ago, he was also a person, and people had hearts. He had given his to her without realizing, long before he'd made any oaths to the Jedi. Seeing her again ten years later had been a revelation and a promise. He had not hesitated to give his heart again, even when she tried, out of duty, to refuse it. When she accepted him, he had never been happier, even though they were in danger of dying. Her love gave him the strength to fight in the arena when all hope seemed gone, and when he lost his hand, hers had helped him while he recovered.

He didn't have R2-D2 with him tonight. He was polite to C-3PO, but clearly had other things on his mind, and the droid didn't linger. Anakin crossed the antechamber, not stopping to admire the view or marvel at the softness of the fabric on the sofa as he might have done before.

She met him in the doorway of her room, ethereal and wondrous, with a smile that he knew was only his.

"Anakin," she said, and threw her arms around his neck.

He would never tire of holding her. She was so small and so fragile. He knew she could take care of herself—he'd seen her do it on more than one occasion—but he would do anything to protect her, anything to keep her safe. He loved her and she loved him, and neither the Senate nor the Jedi could keep them apart. He would not allow it.

"You always crush me when you get here," she said, laughing.

"It's because I'm so in love," he said, but he loosened his hold.

She pressed a kiss to his mouth, her touch light and beautiful, just as she was. She took his hand and led him over to the chair by the window.

"Sit with me for a while?" she asked.

He sensed a wave of sadness from her then. It wasn't related to him, not exactly, so he didn't press the issue. They were still figuring out precisely how they fit together, and living separately didn't help. He tried to give her as much space as she needed, even though he wasn't exactly sure what that was. There was no one he could ask about it, except maybe his stepbrother, and Anakin wasn't sure he wanted to go down that road. If it was a problem, he would solve it later.

He sat down on the wide cushion and leaned back against the pillows. Padmé kicked off the light slippers she was wearing and tucked her feet under her as she curled up at his side. He pulled a coverlet around her, even though he wasn't sure if she was cold. It was the polite thing to do, and she had done it for him more than once.

"This is perfect," he said when they were settled. "I think."

"It's on my short list," Padmé agreed. "I didn't think I could ever be this happy on Coruscant."

"I make you happy?" Anakin knew that already, but it still delighted him.

"Of course you do," Padmé said. "That's why I married you."

"I thought it was for all the thrilling adventure," Anakin drawled.

"After the week I had, I could use fewer thrills, I think," Padmé told him.

"You may have come to the wrong place," Anakin told her seriously. With his arm around her, he could almost reach her bare feet.

"This is my house," she protested, but was cut off as Anakin began to tickle her.

Her giggles were quiet enough that Anakin wasn't worried about anyone overhearing them. She tried to fight him off, but between her laughter and his strength, she didn't stand a chance. They were both breathing hard when he finally relented, and she smacked him on the shoulder as soon as she had some control back.

"That was not very gentlemanly of you," she told him. Her face was flushed.

"I didn't come here to be a gentleman," he said.

She blushed even deeper.

"You're making fun of me again," she said. "I thought you were too scared to make fun of a senator."

"Not when the senator is my wife," he said. He pulled her into his lap. "Then all bets are off."

"I like that word," she said softly. "Husband, wife."

"I say them as often as I can," he confessed. "Even when I'm by myself at the Temple."

This time, her lips lingered on his, pressing lightly but surely against him as she breathed him in. His hands trailed up her back to tangle in her hair. He would never give this up. He could never.

They sat, staring out at the city lights of Coruscant, until the faint pink light of dawn touched the horizon, driving back the dark.

Once there was a girl with a heart and lungs and a planet she wanted to rule, and destiny said she could only pick one. On the top of the mountain, she chose: Her planet first. Her people first. Her world, first.

They gave her a chest piece to process air and move her blood around. Healing took a long, long time, but she lived, and she grew strong again as she got better. Her world loved her. "She will be our queen," they said. "She has given us her heart and the very air she breathes."

She learned the politics of Alderaan and the etiquette of the Great Houses. She found a boy who loved her enough to take her name, forsaking his own legacy forever in the shadow of hers. Together, they kept the planet strong. She took care of the people, and he, risen to the Senate, made sure the galaxy never forgot what Alderaan could offer.

She didn't know how to fight a war.

Alderaan could pay for almost anything, but she knew that credits alone wouldn't get the job done. The Grand Army of the Republic was made up entirely of clone troopers, but they still needed support craft and supply ships. Alderaan mobilized, not for war, exactly—though they would fight if they had to—but for aid.

They didn't send just money to planets the Separatists had ravaged. They sent doctors and teachers and architects. They didn't send just supplies when whole cities were laid waste. They sent builders and medics and droids.

While her husband argued policy on Coruscant, she sent her people into the streets of dangerous places where they were needed most. Some of them never came home, but their families did not blame her. She had sacrificed, too, and they knew that, when she had to, she would sacrifice again.

The heart of Alderaan had changed. It was still a peaceful planet with no large weaponry to speak of, but it was organized. The ships in the royal fleet had more teeth; their officers had seen more hardship.

The lungs of Alderaan had changed. They still made art and lived for beauty, but they manufactured more practical items now, and in larger quantities. The people were still dreamers, but their dreams stretched beyond the limits of the atmosphere.

The world of Alderaan had changed. It was still a beautiful place that hid treacherous cliffs and forgotten crevasses, but it was quietly filling up. Refugees from all over the Republic came there to find their way again, or to stay. It was more cosmopolitan, more creative. More dangerous to those who stood for evil.

The change happened so slowly that no one really noticed, no one in the light and no one in the dark. But it did change. It grew into something the galaxy was going to need, though no one knew that yet, either. And at the center of all of it was the girl.

Breha Organa built something incredible, and in doing so, she laid the foundation for someone who would be even more.

ACKNOWLEDGMENTS

I feel like we've moved a mountain. After twenty years of waiting, not only did we get one Padmé story, we got THREE. And that's thanks to you, gentle readers. Your support has meant everything to me during this trilogy (TRILOGY!!!), and I am so glad we got to do this together.

Josh, compared to the first two, this one was almost normal! You didn't have to figure out what time zone I was in or anything. Thank you for your continued championing of my books. What should we do next?

Jen, it must be said, was ENDLESSLY patient with me on this. I missed every deadline. I handed in the shortest manuscript EVER. I forgot how to spell the names of characters I made up, with alarming consistency. And yet she never gave up on me or made me feel like I was failing. Thank you for shepherding this book, for precise instructions when my brain needed them, and for understanding that some days I was a total wreck. We did it. Eventually.

Emma Higinbotham, Anna-Marie McLemore, and Dot Hutchison were all excellent members of team "I can't explain anything, but I have some questions." Friends who can help you out AND not infringe on your NDA are a real bonus in this business.

Tara Phillips and Leigh Zieske have once again come together with OUTSTANDING cover art and design. These two have done SUCH GOOD WORK on this series, and I love them both so much.

As always, without Story Group I would be afloat on a sea of [Pablo, I need a planet]s. In particular, I would like to thank Emily Shkoukani, who invested a lot of personal time in making sure I had built the characters I wanted to.

Lastly, I want to thank my readers. When *Queen's Peril* came out last June, I had a pretty bad time of it, and you were all amazing. Writing is my job, but I like it the most when I'm having fun, and you make sure that I do. I can't wait to see you again.